DANGEROUS PRETENCE

Elaine hadn't wanted to go back to France, where less than a year ago her marriage had crashed so disastrously; certainly she hadn't wanted to be forced into the company of her husband Yvan. But her uncle Armand was ill and she had no choice. And then she found herself forced into pretending that she and Yvan had become reconciled . . .

Books you will enjoy
by FLORA KIDD

JUNGLE OF DESIRE

It was largely her fault, Diana knew, that her marriage to Jason Clarke had foundered, after a few months. Now, in Ecuador, the two of them had met again. In these exotic surroundings, would they be able to rebuild their marriage—or would the new problems of this different life wreck it for ever?

THE BLACK KNIGHT

When Sandy first set eyes on the dark, unsmiling Lymond Caldwell, he reminded her of a knight of olden days. Knightlike, too, he seemed to be constantly rescuing her from some predicament or other. But she must beware of being too grateful to him—for to fall in love would be a disaster.

THE BARGAIN BRIDE

Lee had gone out to Curaçao to marry one man, but soon found herself married to another—the inscrutable Max Van Breedan. It was a marriage of convenience on both sides—so why did Lee find herself so deeply resenting Beatrix Deering, the woman Max *would* have married had she been free?

THE SUMMER WIFE

Deirdre had married Rory Mallon because he had lost his sight temporarily, and only a wife could help him finish the work he was doing. Soon she had fallen in love with him. But Deirdre was plain, while all the other women in his life had been beautiful. What would happen when he recovered his sight?

DANGEROUS PRETENCE

BY

FLORA KIDD

MILLS & BOON LIMITED
17–19 FOLEY STREET
LONDON W1A 1DR

First published 1977
Philippine copyright 1977
This edition 1977

ISBN 0 263 72480 8

Made and printed in Great Britain by
Richard Clay (The Chaucer Press), Ltd., Bungay, Suffolk

CHAPTER ONE

When she received the news that her great-uncle Armand St Vérain was very ill and asking for her to visit him at his country house in Chambourtin-en-Duvay, France, Elaine Cooper first made sure she could have a day off from her work in the offices of a well-known wine-importer in the city of London, looked up the times of departure of flights from London to Paris and then sat down to write and tell Marguerite, Armand's wife, that she would be arriving at Charles de Gaulle Airport at ten o'clock on Friday morning.

Her plane landed on time, and after collecting her suitcase from the luggage carousel Elaine looked around to see if anyone had come to meet her. She did not see anyone she recognised, so she waited for a while. After fifteen minutes when no one came forward to greet her she decided to hire a car and drive herself to Chambourtin, and soon she was at the wheel of a small red Renault, weaving in and out of the Paris traffic on her way to the Route Nationale which delves down through the French countryside to the cities of Chartres, Tours and Poitiers and into the plains of Aquitaine.

Since she enjoyed driving and was familiar with the way she made good time, and at Chartres she paused to take coffee at an old *auberge* in the main square. There was a temptation to linger and walk up to the towered cathedral; but she wanted to be in Chambourtin by at least four o'clock, so she drove on along the straight sunny highway, delighting in glimpses of ancient churches dominating small villages of old lop-sided houses, of gardens where roses bloomed in profusion and of distant white-walled chateaux glimmering beside smooth blue-reflecting rivers. Beyond Tours she stopped in a quiet village to sit at a round painted iron table outside a *bistro* and eat a crisp roll of French bread crammed with succulent pink ham. Relaxing for a while under the shade of an old chestnut tree, she sipped ice-cold lemonade through a straw before continuing on her way.

By the time she was approaching Poitiers the road was infested with lorries and Elaine had to keep her wits about her. She came to the city suddenly over the rim of a ravine in which one of the two rivers ran. Across a bridge she drove and the city rose up before her, a natural fortress built on a rocky promontory. Changing gear, she flung the car at a steep street, swung it through the market place past the beautiful Romanesque church of Ste Marie la Grande, its great doorway flanked by two little lantern turrets with pine-cone-roofing, then down to another bridge and out into the country again with the great plain rolling away before her, shadowed only by small white clouds which floated lazily across the blue sky.

Half-way between Poitiers and Angoulême she turned off down a narrow country lane which passed through villages that were immemorially old. The slanting rays of the westering sun gilded crumbling medieval walls and weather-worn sagging roofs. It also glinted on the red and yellow of highly polished farm machinery working in well-tended fields. A group of primeval standing stones, gaunt and mysterious, shared a meadow with Charollais cattle which, pug-nosed and heavily-quartered, grazed placidly amongst wild mustard and white daisies. In a farmyard tiny goats leapt about a young girl as she threw meal to them from a basket. In another yard fine white geese waddled to a pond.

On and on she drove in the hot afternoon sunshine, always south-westwards, and when the road dipped down to run beside a wide placid river Elaine felt that leap of joy which comes when something familiar comes into sight. For the river was the Duvay. Tall Lombardy poplars marched along its banks and their shadows made slanting black stripes across the sun-bright surface of the road.

To Elaine the soldier-straight line of trees was a link with all the other times she had travelled this road as a child in the company of her grandmother Eleanor St Vérain Cooper—that indefatigable Frenchwoman who, after Elaine's parents had been killed in a car crash, had brought her granddaughter every summer for eight years to the old chateau set among the vineyards which in their time had produced some of the best brandy ever to come out of the Charente district of France.

Now she was almost home. She was in the deep, deep country where there was no other car in sight; none, that is, until she glanced warily in the rear-view mirror and felt a tingle of apprehension when she saw yet again the big grey Citroën coming up behind her, its chromium-plated fittings seeming to gleam menacingly through the cloud of dust that its wheels stirred up on the summer-dry road.

While she had been on the Route Nationale the frequent presence of a grey Citroën behind her had not alarmed her. After all, France was full of grey Citroëns, and it might not have always been the same one. But by the time she had reached Poitiers she had begun to be suspicious, for no matter how often other cars came between her and the grey car it always appeared again, keeping its distance tauntingly so that she was never able to make out the numbers on its licence plate nor see whether the driver was a woman or a man.

Once again she flicked a glance at the mirror. The sight of the car following her along this country road, still keeping its distance even though it had the power and the opportunity to overtake her, gave her an uneasy feeling that its driver knew who she was and was taking an almost sadistic pleasure in staying behind her to torment her.

Elaine's soft mouth tightened and her dark brown eyes narrowed. The behaviour of the grey car reminded her of someone; someone she had not expected to see until she arrived at the chateau, someone she had managed to avoid seeing for almost nine months —her husband, Yvan Durocher, whom she had left after only four months of marriage because she had learned that he had been unfaithful to her.

She took a long shuddering breath, because remembrance of what had happened last year still had power to hurt her. How gullible she had been, how foolishly romantic, for allowing herself to be swept off her feet by a cold-hearted, practical Frenchman for whom marriage was only a convenience!

Hate for Yvan and for how he had humiliated her surged through her in a hot flood. Hardly realising what she was doing, intent only on getting away from the grey car which was following her so relentlessly, she put her foot on the accelerator. The little red car responded immediately and leaped forward as a rat leaps away from a big cat which has been stalking it.

Loose chips lying on the surface of the tarmac,

which had not long been laid, spat from under the rapidly revolving tyres. The road curved away to the left to follow a bend in the river. Too late Elaine realised the car was travelling too fast to take the bend easily, and the wheels mounted the shoulder of the road. She tried to brake, again too late, and carried by its own momentum the car plunged down the slippery dry grass of a bank and came to a rest in the dried-up ditch.

Shaken but not hurt, Elaine switched off the engine of the car, then leaned her forehead against the steering wheel for a few moments in an attempt to control the trembling caused by the shock of the accident. Her thick waving gold-coloured hair slid forward and hid her face from the view of the man who had left his car parked on the roadside came down the bank and approached the Renault. He wrenched open the door.

'*Qu'est-ce qui arrive, madame?* What happened?' His voice was deep and slow. Yvan's voice, which she had tried so hard to forget. 'Are you all right?' he added when she didn't move, and there was just a touch of concern in his tone.

But she still didn't move or answer him. Now that she was sure who had been following her the urge to torment him in turn was overwhelming. Let him think for a while that she was hurt or possibly dead! Perhaps he might feel a twinge of conscience.

She heard him mutter a French curse, then felt his hands hard and firm on her shoulders. At once a feeling compounded of delight and fear stabbed through her. She had not realised his touch would have such a devastating effect on her after all these months, and she had to resist a desperate urge to wrench free.

Slowly he pulled her away from the steering wheel until she lay against the back of the seat. Eyes closed, she waited for him to react to the sight of her. After a few seconds when nothing happened and all she could hear was the chirping of crickets in the long grass, the singing of birds and the perpetual rustle of poplar leaves, she decided to groan a little and allow her eyelashes to lift just enough to show that she was alive and coming round.

'You look very beautiful lying there, *ma chère femme,* but you don't fool me. You have too much colour in your face to be unconscious or hurt.'

There was no note of concern in the deep voice now. It had a hard caustic edge to it and his mocking reference to their relationship flicked her on the raw. Opening her dark brown eyes which were so unusual with her fair English colouring, Elaine sat up and glared at him.

He was leaning against the inside of the open car door and from under level dark eyebrows his indigo blue eyes were watching her with an expression of derision glinting in them. Nothing seemed changed about him. His rough black hair, prematurely streaked here and there with grey, still had a tendency to wave and was still long enough at the back to touch the collar of his shirt. His lean face still had a tanned leathery look about it, due to the hours he spent out of doors under a hot sun. And his wide mouth still had that provocative sensual curve which had made her wonder, when she had first met him, what it would be like to be kissed by him.

Without a jacket, he was wearing a shirt of clinging cotton knit which emphasised the bulge of muscle in his shoulders and chest. It was short-sleeved and its creamy colour contrasted sharply with the deep tan of his brawny arms. A pair of blue and fawn checked trousers belted at the waist were moulded closely to his powerful thighs and flared out slightly towards his feet. As always his tough physique, combined with the aquiline cast of his features and the grace of his long-fingered hands, added up to an impression of earthiness and sophistication; a dangerously attractive mixture, as she knew only too well.

'Why have you been following me?' she challenged, taking the initiative.

'Have I been following you?' Yvan countered coolly, and for a moment she was disconcerted. Perhaps he had been only to Poitiers on an errand and just happened to be returning. Then she saw derision glint in his eyes again and saw his mouth quirk at one corner and knew she was right. He had followed her all the way.

'Of course you have,' she asserted. 'You've sat on my tail deliberately to ... to torment me.' She broke off when she saw his mouth widen in a smile, an unexpectedly sweet smile in the tough tanned face as he leaned forward suddenly to stroke one long finger down her cheek.

'How well you know me, *chérie*,' he derided softly. 'Isn't there a saying "better the devil you know than the devil you don't know"? Perhaps you should think about it during the next few days you are at the chateau.'

'I'm not staying long,' she retorted, flinching away from his caressing finger and cringing against the back of the seat, her big brown eyes wide under the finely plucked arching eyebrows; wide with something very close to fear because it seemed he had guessed at her real reason for coming. 'I have to be back at work on Monday,' she added determinedly.

'We shall see,' he replied calmly, and at once she was on guard. She knew how inflexible he could be when he had made up his mind to follow a certain course of action.

'I'm not staying any longer, Yvan,' she said. 'You can't make me.'

He didn't enter into argument with her but merely shrugged his shoulders.

'*Et maintenant,* since you're not hurt in any way may I suggest you continue the rest of your journey with me? I doubt very much whether your car can be removed from that ditch without the help of proper equipment,' he said smoothly.

Suddenly anxious about the car, Elaine scrambled out of it and pushed past him to go and examine its position in the ditch. There didn't seem to be any damage to the bodywork as far as she could see, but when she turned and looked at the steep slope of the bank she realised that Yvan was right. The car could only be raised up out of the ditch by a small crane.

She became aware that he had slammed the door of the car shut and had walked round to the back of the vehicle. He was actually opening the boot with the keys which he had presumably taken from the ignition. Feeling indignation rising inside her, she walked round to his side.

'Just what do you think you're doing?' she demanded.

'Taking your suitcase out of the boot,' he replied aggravatingly, suiting his action to his words. 'I expect there are clothes in it that you'll be needing.'

'Leave it alone,' she ordered sharply. 'You have no right to touch it or to tell me what to do!'

He slammed the boot shut and, her case in his hand, he turned to give her a mocking glance.

'*Au contraire, chérie,*' he retorted calmly. 'I have every right to look after you and your property and to tell you what to do. I am still your husband.'

Side-stepping round her, he lunged up the slope in a few strides. Elaine followed him slipping and sliding in the dry stiff grass and reeds. By the time she reached the top of the slope she was breathless and her case was in the boot of the Citroën, which was firmly closed and locked.

'*Allons!*' ordered Yvan, striding round to open the front door on the driver's side.

'Wait ... I've left my handbag in the Renault,' she exclaimed hastily, and returned down the slope, her cautious steps developing into a precipitous run which only ended against the Renault. Pulling at the door, she found it wouldn't open and realised that Yvan had locked it for safety. She glanced round exasperatedly and was just in time to catch the keys which he threw to her.

She collected her handbag from the Renault's front seat, locked the door again and started back up the slope, wishing she was wearing anything but the high-heeled sling-back beige sandals which went so well with the green and beige dress of silky knit material she was wearing. She reflected ruefully that she was dressed more for a day out in Paris than a day in the country.

The engine of the Citroën was ticking over quietly and Yvan was sitting at the steering wheel smoking a cigarette. Elaine opened the door and slid into the seat beside him. The door was hardly closed when the car moved forward and as they sped along the road the shadows of the poplars flicked over it.

'We'll stop at the petrol station this side of the village,' said Yvan. 'Marcel has a tow truck with a crane. He'll be glad to haul the Renault out of the ditch for you, I've no doubt. Always when I call in for petrol he asks about you, wonders when you're coming back to Chambourtin.'

Elaine gnawed at her lower lip and looked out of the windscreen. In the distance the houses of the village of Chambourtin shimmered like a mirage across the flat fields which surrounded it, and beyond them the spire of St Augustine, where she had been married, rose slim and graceful from a clump of dark cypresses. The sight of the spire and the mention that Marcel Daudet, the fatherly proprietor of the local garage, had been asking for her touched her in a way she had not expected. Already, it seemed, Chambourtin was beginning to exert its spell, making her feel she belonged there and should have never gone away.

But she mustn't let that happen. She must resist all attempts by people and places to trap her here, above all she must resist any attempt by the man she was sitting beside to trap her in a relationship which had turned sour on her. So she didn't get out of the Citroën when it pulled up in the cluttered yard in front of the big shed where Marcel and his son Claude repaired car engines, motor-cycles and bicycles. Instead she sat hot and sullen staring out at the Daudet house, a typical modern French home, plain and square. Only the frilled curtains curving at the windows and the flower boxes foaming with marigolds, gillyflowers and asters softened the austerity of the exterior of the house, she was thinking, when the sound of laughter drew her attention away from it and in the direction of Yvan and the swarthy Marcel.

They were looking in her direction and she was sure they were laughing about her. Probably Yvan had been telling Marcel about how she had driven off the road into the ditch, exaggerating the incident a little, dressing it up with sardonic humour calculated to raise a laugh. Tossing her head, she looked away from them, only to find hot tears pricking her eyes as she realised that Yvan cared so little for her he could crack jokes about her with the garage proprietor.

But suddenly there was Marcel himself at the window of the car, smiling and nodding at her in his kindly way. It would be unkind of her not to let the window down further and speak to him.

'*Bonjour, mademoiselle ... ah, excusez-moi ... Bonjour, madame*. It is good to see you again,' he said.

'*Bonjour, monsieur*,' she replied. His obvious pleasure in this meeting warmed her, and she could not help smiling at him. 'It's good to be here,' she heard herself saying, much to her surprise. 'I hope you'll take care of the hired car for me and bring it to the chateau as soon as you can.'

Marcel beamed. 'It will be a pleasure, *madame*, just as it was when I used to take care of your bicycle when it had a puncture. You remember those days, eh? When you used to cycle into the village from the chateau to buy your ice cream from Madame Sorel?'

'Yes, I remember,' replied Elaine. 'How is Madame Sorel?'

'Not good, not good,' he answered, shaking his head. 'She is in the hospital now in Cognac.'

'Oh, I'm sorry.'

'My wife and I shall be visiting her tomorrow. I shall tell her you are back, she will be pleased. *Au revoir, madame*.'

He stepped back and touched his hand to his forehead in an old-fashioned salute as the car moved forward with Yvan once more behind the steering wheel. Along the narrow winding street they drove, where the deep summer shadows of ancient tiled roofs shaded the upper windows of old houses in front of which bright bunches of crimson phlox and purple asters blazed against the pale gold of the unshadowed stone of the lower storeys.

Before they reached the Romanesque church with its rounded arches and delicate carvings the road turned sharply left over a stone bridge with three arches which were reflected in smooth blue water. On the other side of the river the road climbed a low hill, leaving the river for a while to twist past thick woods.

'How is Uncle Armand?' Elaine asked, unable to keep quiet for long.

'He is dying.' The answer went through her like a knife and again she felt the prick of tears in her eyes.

'And your mother?'

'At his side, as a good wife should be when her husband is ill . . . so she tells me.'

The final sardonic remark was a taunt aimed at her, she knew, a comment on the fact that she had run away from him last year. She glanced sideways, saw the cynical curve of his mouth and felt an unexpected twinge of remorse as she realised that her own behaviour was the cause of his cynicism.

She looked out at the rolling countryside again and thought about Marguerite, his mother and Armand's wife, and recalled her grandmother's exclamation of dismay when the news came that at the age of sixty-five, after remaining a bachelor until that point in his life, Armand St Vérain had married Marguerite Durocher, his housekeeper and the widow of Jean Durocher who for many years had been the superintendent of the St Vérain vineyards.

'*Mon dieu,*' Eleanor had exclaimed, 'he is out of his mind! There is only one consolation. She is past child-bearing age.'

All of which had meant nothing to Elaine, who at

the age of twelve was not in the least interested in the complications of the lives of adults. But that summer she had not gone to Chambourtin for her summer holidays, because her grandmother had been stricken down by a severe stroke which had paralysed her and confined her to hospital, where she had died some weeks later.

Suddenly homeless, Elaine had been taken in by her father's cousin, Charles Cooper, managing director of the old established vintners Cooper and Downes. For the next eight years she had not visited Chambourtin, although she had written regularly and dutifully to her great-uncle, writing her letters in the French which her grandmother had taught her to speak and write and which she had continued to learn at the school she had attended with Charles' two daughters. It wasn't that she hadn't wanted to visit the old man and the chateau, but her holidays always seemed to be arranged for her and it had been much more fun, or so she had thought in her teens, to go with her cousins on trips to the Highlands of Scotland or on sailing cruises among the Greek Islands.

It hadn't been until she was twenty-one and working in the offices of Cooper and Downes that she had decided to accept an urgent invitation from her uncle to go to Chambourtin again. She had come, driving down in a hired car as she had today, almost exactly a year ago and for the first time in her life she had met Yvan Durocher, who had taken over his father's job as manager of the vineyard. And she had fallen in love with him.

The road lifted over another low hill and there was the river again. It had swept round in a big curve from the bridge and was edged by willows and aspens. Above it, set among lawns and woodland, was the small yet elegant chateau of Chambourtin, the pointed roof of its single tower topped by a brass weather-vane that twinkled in the sunlight. Beyond the house the land rolled away to a distant horizon which edged like a hem of blue the green vineyards, bright meadows and dark woods.

'It's so lovely!' she exclaimed involuntarily, feeling once again the special attraction which the place had for her. Was it because she possessed a little of the St Vérain blood in her veins that it spoke to her? For hundreds of years the St Vérains had owned this land and had cultivated it meticulously, laying out the vineyards according to the nature of the soil from *grand champagne* and *petit champagne* to the *bois communs*. It was part of the wide territory that had been developed especially for the brandy industry, and perhaps Elaine should not be surprised because she felt the pull of heritage whenever she saw it.

The car slowed down and was guided into a small layby where tourists often stopped their cars to take a picnic and admire the view.

'If you think it's so lovely why did you leave and say you would never return?' Yvan asked casually as he turned off the engine.

'You know why,' she replied, feeling the perspiration bead her brow suddenly. Now that the car had stopped the interior of it was very hot and there was no shelter from the bright hot rays of the sun which blazed in through the windscreen. 'I wrote and told you why. I can't live there while you're there. I can't live with you as your wife. Oh, Yvan, why not admit the reality of the situation? You and I just don't have the same attitude to marriage...'

'*Mais, c'est vrai,*' he interrupted her roughly. 'For you it is something you did on the impulse of the moment because you felt like it, because the summer sun, the roses and the wine put you in the mood; something you believed you could end a few months later if you found you didn't like it.'

'Oh! Well, what about you? Didn't you marry for convenience and think you could make certain of your future if you married the one person who might inherit Chambourtin vineyards?' she burst out furiously, cut to the quick by his implication that she had behaved irresponsibly by marrying him. 'But you made a mistake. You assumed I'd be like one of your placid French wives, content to stay at home to cook the meals and dust the furniture while you ... you looked for pleasure in the bed of another woman!'

He had been looking out of the wide window while she was speaking, but as she paused to regain her breath he turned his head slowly to look at her. He raised one eyebrow in sardonic amusement and the curve of his mouth mocked her.

'So,' he drawled, 'we get to the heart of the matter at last. In your letters you didn't mention another woman as one of your reasons for deserting me.'

'I didn't desert you,' she denied shakily.

'Oh, come now, let's not quibble over words. You left me, and when I wrote and suggested you return you refused. I believe that is called desertion. Perhaps now you'll be good enough to tell me the name of the woman ...' he paused, then added with wicked mockery of her accent, 'in whose bed I'm supposed to have found pleasure during the months you and I lived together.'

Laughter shook his voice as if he found the whole matter highly diverting. Unable to sustain his mocking gaze, Elaine tilted her chin and looked out of the windscreen again.

'Solange Bourget,' she said.

'And who told you?'

'She did.'

'And you believed her?' Now he sounded astounded as well as amused.

'Oh, stop laughing at me!' she stormed, turning on him. 'Knowing your reputation with women before we married I didn't find it difficult to believe her.'

She sat tensely, watching a wasp which had flown in through the open window blunder against the windscreen in an effort to get out and felt sweat break out again on her skin as she waited half-hopefully for Yvan to deny Solange's claim that he had continued to be her lover after his marriage. But he said nothing, and once again she had to break an uneasy silence.

'May we go on now to the chateau?' she asked.

'Not yet.'

He sighed rather wearily and she looked at him. Mockery had gone from his face. His large heavy-lidded dark eyes considered her sombrely for a moment, then he turned to reach into the back seat for the blue blazer jacket that was lying on it. He took a packet of cigarettes from the pocket and threw the jacket back on to the seat. He offered her a cigarette, but knowing they would be French and not to her taste she shook her head in refusal, watched him select one, put it in his mouth and light it. Almost as if she were mesmerised her eyes followed the lighter as he returned it to his trouser pocket. It wasn't the same one that he had used nine months ago.

'I have something to tell you,' he said after he had taken a few draws on the cigarette. 'Yesterday I drove up to Paris with the intention of staying the night there and going to meet you off the early plane so that I could discuss a matter of some importance with you while we drove here. It still waits to be discussed.'

'You went to meet me? Then why weren't you at the airport?'

His smile was crooked, a little bleak, and seemed to mock himself.

'I stayed the night with an old friend, and we sat up drinking cognac and reminiscing. I drank too much and overslept this morning. By the time I reached the airport your plane had landed and you'd gone. I inquired at the car rental agencies and found you had rented a red Renault. You were well beyond the outskirts of Paris on your way to Chartres, driving too fast as usual, before I was able to catch up with you.'

'But if you wanted to talk to me why didn't you overtake me and stop me?' she asked.

Yvan shrugged his big shoulders and made a gesture with his long-fingered hands.

'You could ask me why I got drunk last night. The answer to both questions would be the same,' he replied rather harshly.

'I don't understand.'

'To explain would be to strip my soul bare, and that's something I won't do for any woman, not even for you, *ma chère femme*,' he retorted dryly.

'Stop calling me that!' she exploded.

'Why? You're still my wife. We aren't divorced, even if we haven't lived together for nearly a year.'

Elaine moved uneasily, pushing back her thick wavy hair. It was when the weather was hot that she thought of having the heavy tresses cut short and shaped to her head in a new style, but always she hesitated. Why? Because this man had once said he liked long hair on a woman.

'Is that what you want to discuss, divorce?' she queried, trying to keep her voice cool and hard.

He rubbed a hand across his brow to wipe off the sweat which had sprung out on his skin.

'It's too damned hot in here to discuss anything,' he muttered evasively. 'Let's get out and walk in the woods.'

Elaine hesitated. Walking through the woods was something they had done often a year ago and many times he had pulled her down to sit beside him on a bank of thick moss. It was there under the arching green of the leaves that he had first kissed her, pushing her back against the soft cushioning moss, parting her lips with his, caressing her body—gently at first and then later when she had responded with delight to the new exciting pleasure he had given her, with a passionate possessiveness that had awoken exquisite yearnings in her for more caresses. In fact it had been those stolen moments of awakening to the joys of physical passion which had led her into believing that she was in love with him and should marry him.

The door beside her was jerked open sharply, pulled by an impatient hand.

'Are you coming?' he asked curtly.

He wasn't even looking at her. He was as withdrawn from her as a stranger might be and it was hard to believe that once they had been intimate and had achieved together the ultimate delight of physical union.

She swung her legs out and stood up. It was a relief to be out of the stuffy car and as they entered the woods the shade of the pale green leaves of the beech trees was like a blessing. Nothing moved in the warm scented air. Not a bird sang and the sound of their footsteps was muffled by the thick mat of last year's dead leaves which still covered the path.

'No doubt you have some idea of how your uncle

regards our separation,' said Yvan abruptly. Hands in his trouser pockets, he walked easily in his crepe-soled suede shoes while she was having difficulty in her high-heeled sandals.

'Yes, I have. He's written to me often about it,' she replied stiffly.

'Then perhaps you know also that he would like very much to see us reconciled?'

'Yes. I do. Your mother said he would like that in the letter she sent to me telling me he was ill and wanted me to visit him. In my reply I told her that a reconciliation between us is impossible.'

'I know that. She gave me the letter to read,' he said brusquely. 'And that's why I had to talk to you before you reached the chateau. He can no longer see to read, so she reads to him. She read your letter, but instead of saying that a reconciliation is impossible she said that it's possible.' He paused, then added with a touch of humour, 'He now believes that it will take place as soon as you set foot in the house this afternoon.'

'Oh, how dare she do that!' exclaimed Elaine, and came to an abrupt stop. 'How dare she meddle in my affairs?'

Yvan stopped walking too and turned to face her, bestriding the narrow path and crossing his arms across his chest.

'Allow me to substitute "our" for "my", and remind you that any reconciliation between us would involve me as well as you,' he cautioned dryly. 'And my mother dares, as you say, because she can't bear to see him distressed any more by your irresponsible behaviour.'

The criticism flicked at her pride, but she wasn't going to let him have the satisfaction of knowing that it had. Raising her eyebrows, she laughed, a little trill of mockery.

'Oh no,' she retorted. 'She's much more likely to have reversed what I wrote in my letter to suit your ambitions.'

In the sun-dappled shade of the woods it wasn't easy to see the expression on his face, but she thought he looked momentarily puzzled.

'This is interesting,' he murmured, 'but I fail to see how a reconciliation with you would suit my ambitions, whatever they may be.'

'Don't tell me you've forgotten why you married me,' she jibed scathingly.

'No, I haven't forgotten,' he said quietly. 'But I'd like to hear your version of why I did.'

'You knew that I was heiress to my uncle's property and you knew that if you married me he might change his will to make you his stepson, co-heir to Chambourtin with me. It follows that if we aren't reconciled he could change his will again and make me sole heir once more.'

He stared at her, his eyes narrow, and rubbed at his chin with one hand. Then he shrugged and his mouth curved tauntingly as a gleam of amusement lit his dark eyes.

'You're very confident that he would change his will in your favour, aren't you?' he scoffed softly, and she felt a chill of apprehension tingle through her.

'Yes, I'm the only person surviving who has St Vérain blood in my veins, and my grandmother once told me...'

'Ah, your grandmother,' he interrupted her with an unpleasant twist to his mouth. 'I've heard all about her and her plotting and conniving and how angry she was when she realised that she'd inherited nothing of

Chambourtin—that it had all been left to her younger brother.'

'That isn't true! She didn't plot and connive. She was very fond of Uncle Armand.'

'*Mais oui*, so fond of him that she came between him and the one woman he loved, and made sure he didn't marry and have children so that her own son—your father—might inherit the place. But her plans were foiled when your father was killed, so she took over your upbringing, brought you here every summer, trained you to ingratiate yourself with your great-uncle so that...'

'I've never ingratiated myself with him,' she almost shouted at him, 'and my grandmother wasn't like that. Oh, how horrible and cynical you are!'

'So I'm horrible and cynical because I present to you a little of the truth?' he jeered. 'But there's more to come. When you ran away nine months ago because you decided you didn't like being married to me, you never considered how your behaviour might look to your great-uncle, did you? You never gave him a thought. You forgot that he is a traditionalist in his beliefs and that for him marriage is a sacred bond between two people which should never be broken by another person. If he hadn't believed that all his life he would have tried to break up my parents' marriage years ago.'

He paused and waited as if he expected her to make some comment, but she was too amazed by what she was hearing about people she had known all her life to think of anything to say.

'I believe that in his own way your uncle has tried hard to save our marriage by writing to you and offering you his advice,' he continued more quietly. 'But you've seen fit to reject his advice and he has been hurt. I expect you don't realise it, but sometimes old people don't take kindly to being slighted as you seem to have slighted him. Sometimes they turn against the person who has injured them. So you could be right. He could be considering a change in his will, but not in your favour. It's just possible that it will be changed in my favour.' Again his mouth took on a sardonic twist. 'Bearing that in mind you'll see that by telling him a reconciliation is possible between us my mother was hardly suiting my ambitions. In short, it's possible that I stand to gain more if we aren't reconciled.'

Stunned by what he had just told her, Elaine could only stand and stare at him. Big and dark, he loomed before her like a sadistic devil sent to punish her for wrongdoing. If she did not agree to end their separation she would pay the penalty and lose her inheritance.

He stepped towards her and made a gesture of conciliation with his hands.

'Now that you're here I thought we could come to some sort of arrangement,' he said gently.

'No, no, I can't. I won't!' she cried, afraid that he might step nearer and touch her. She whirled away, intent on running back to the car. She knew he had left the keys in it—if she could reach it before he caught up with her she might be able to start it and drive to the village. But her high heels let her down. She went sprawling to jar one knee painfully against an exposed tree root. Her hands went out instinctively to break her fall and clutched at the soft moss.

Gasping for breath, she began to scramble to her feet, then felt a hand grasp her arm and haul her up. Turning, she tried to wrench herself free and couldn't.

'Let go of me!' she panted, but the hand only tightened bruisingly. Desperately she tried to twist free, her body writhing, her hair swinging across her face in rippling waves. Yvan gave her arm a sharp pull and pain twisted agonisingly in her shoulder as she was jerked against his hard body. With his other hand he imprisoned her other arm and, held like that against his chest, she glared up at him mutinously through the strands of bright hair which straggled over her eyes.

'The time has come for you to stop running from your responsibilities, you selfish little coward,' he grated. 'Since my mother told your uncle that we're to be reconciled his mental condition has improved. He's looking forward to seeing you. For you to blunder into his room and say that a reconciliation is impossible would set him back, possibly hasten his death. That's why I had to talk to you before you reached the house, to warn you.'

'Oh, don't bother to explain,' she said in a low, furious voice, 'I can guess what you're going to say. But I haven't come here to be reconciled with you. I want a divorce and nothing, not even the possibility of being cut out of his will, is going to make me change my mind.' She drew a shuddering breath and cried out, 'Oh, can't you see I hate you?'

'I can see I stir up some violent emotion in you, which I suppose is preferable to indifference,' he mocked. 'But I wasn't about to suggest you change your mind about me.'

Elaine swallowed nervously, shook the hair out of her eyes and tried once again to pull away from him, without success. The warmth of his body was beginning to penetrate through their clothing to her body and she could smell the well-remembered scents of his clean sun-bronzed skin. His hands moved slightly on the bare skin of her arms and the feel of them, roughened by his work, against the smoothness of her skin roused a sensuousness within her, a longing to touch him, to slide her fingers within the opening of his shirt and caress the warm hairiness of his chest, the taut line of his throat, and awake the passion which slumbered just below his outwardly calm exterior.

'What were you going to suggest, then?' she mumbled, turning her head away from him, keeping herself rigid in his hold as she resisted temptation.

'That we pretend we're reconciled,' he replied coolly.

'Pretend?' She was shocked and showed it in her loud exclamation, in the wide-eyed glance she gave him.

'*Oui.* We could pretend for a while just to ease the last days of an old man who has tried to do his best for us both, who had loved you and treated you as if you were his daughter and not the only grandchild of his much older sister.' The hard hands left her arms suddenly. Yvan stepped away from her and made a lifting gesture with his hands as if offering her a gift. 'I put it to you, is it too much to ask you to do this for Armand? Are you so taken up with your own feelings that you can't push them aside and consider his?'

No longer held captive, Elaine didn't run away but stood rubbing one arm above the elbow, trying to smooth away the soreness caused by his fingers. She wasn't selfish, at least not deliberately so, and she had always loved the gentle delicate Armand who had taught her how to appreciate art and music as well as telling her a little about the fascinating history of this part of France, which at one time had been ruled over by a duchess who had also been Queen of England, Eleanor of Aquitaine.

Her first impulse then was to agree with Yvan's suggestion, to reach out a hand to him and say, 'Let's go now and show Uncle Armand we're together.' But just recently impulsive action had led her into difficulties, so she hesitated and searched his face for some clue to his feelings. His profile was dark and impassive. Perhaps there was a touch of weariness in the way he waited for her reply, as with his hands once more thrust into his trouser pockets he pushed at a mound of dead leaves with the toe of one shoe.

Why had he made such a suggestion? she wondered. How could it possibly benefit him if they pretended to be reconciled? Knowing him to be essentially practical by nature she couldn't accept that his motives in making such a suggestion were entirely unselfish. And if what he had told her about the possibility of her uncle changing his will in his favour if they weren't reconciled was true, it wouldn't benefit him at all ... except that it would mean that the will as it was would still stand. He would be co-heir with her. They would have to share Chambourtin between them as they had once shared a bed.

'No,' she said, her voice ringing out clearly in the silence of the woods, 'it's asking too much of me. I can't do it.'

The words were hardly uttered when she was swamped by an overwhelming feeling of shame because she would not, after all, forget her own feelings to make easy the last days of an old man who had always been kind to her. The shame burned in her cheeks and she covered them with her hands, hiding them from the scorn which was expressed in the dark eyes which glanced at her from under frowning black eyebrows.

Seconds passed in fragrant sunlit silence. She heard Yvan move and braced herself for his anger, letting her hands fall to her sides. But he merely shrugged his shoulders as he turned away from her.

'Then there's no more to be said,' he drawled indifferently. 'Shall we go on to the house? Or would you prefer to return to the village now that you know what's in store for you? You could wait at Marcel's for your car so that you would turn tail again on your responsibilities and run back to England.'

Disgust thickened his voice and the sarcasm seared her like the flicker of a flame. A new suspicion leapt into her mind which was so ready to be suspicious of him. Was it possible he didn't want her to go to the chateau? Did he hope she would run away again? That would certainly suit his ends.

'I want to go to the chateau. After all, I promised I'd come,' she replied, and again he shrugged as if it were a matter of indifference to him what she decided to do.

'Then let's go,' he murmured, and began to stride back along the path.

CHAPTER TWO

STILL bothered by Yvan's indifferent acceptance of her refusal to pretend she was reconciled with him, Elaine followed him back along the path which wound through the silent woods. As she stepped out of the shade the heat of the sun's rays hit her like a blast from a furnace and when she approached the car she was alarmed at the reflection of herself in the back side window. It would never do, she realised, to arrive at the chateau with her hair in such wild disorder. A glance down at her legs showed her that her sheer nylon tights had been ripped by her fall.

Yvan was walking round the back of the car to the driver's seat, so after a quick glance to make sure no other car was coming in either direction Elaine lifted the skirt of her dress and with a few sinuous movements pulled the tights down over her hips and legs. She felt cooler without them anyway, she thought as she removed one foot at a time from them and thrust her bare feet back into her sandals.

'Ready now?' Yvan sounded amused and she looked up to find he had been watching her over the top of the car.

'I shall be when I've combed my hair,' she retorted.

'You can do that as we drive along,' he replied. 'We're late already and my mother will be thinking that some accident has happened to us.'

She wanted to retort that it wasn't her fault they were late and that she didn't care whether his mother was worried or not, but another glance at his impassive, indifferent face as he opened the car door made her realise that ranting at him would be a waste of time and breath.

It always had been, she thought ruefully, as she took her place beside him in the car, and remembered the few times she had lost her temper with him last year and had flung words at him. He had never flung any back but had let her rant until she had stopped for want of breath. Then he had said something quiet and reasonable about a different subject, not bothering either to defend himself or to attack her, and had always made her feel as if she had made a great deal of fuss about nothing. And in a way, that ability of his for turning the other cheek and refusing to be drawn into a quarrel had made her a little afraid of him.

The car moved forward again and she took a mirror from her handbag and examined her appearance in it. Heavens, how flushed and wild she looked! Being thick and wavy her hair was always difficult to control, and her recent struggle with Yvan had caused it to coil into snake-like ringlets which stood out from her head so that she looked like a picture of the Medusa she had once seen in a book of Greek myths.

Her eyes had an angry light in them, her nose was shining and, without the soft sheen of lipstick, her lips looked dry. It would never do for the meticulous Marguerite St Vérain to see her looking like this, so she set to work with comb, compact and lipstick. By the time the car turned through an archway between two long stone buildings called *chais*, where brandy had once been stored, and swept into the courtyard at the back of the house, Elaine looked as cool and composed as it was possible to look on that hot end-of-August day.

The purple of petunias, the orange and yellow of

nasturtiums and the scarlet of geraniums blazed in profusion and tumbled from window boxes and hanging baskets, their brilliance offset by the virginia creeper which shimmered like a green cascade down the walls of the house. As she stepped from the car Elaine smelt again the rich scent of roses and wine, a scent she always associated with staying at the chateau.

For a moment she stood looking up at the house. It was L-shaped and at the corner of the L, linking the two wings together, was the square tower built one storey higher than the rest of the house. It had a big arched doorway, and even while she hesitated one of the double doors under the arch opened and a grey-haired man appeared and stepped into the courtyard towards her, his broad face breaking into a smile. He was Jacques, who had been butler at the house for many years.

'*Bonjour, madame,*' he greeted her. 'You are very welcome. We were beginning to think something had happened to delay you. Let me take that, *monsieur*.' He reached out a hand to take her suitcase from Yvan. 'I will take it up to your room for you, *madame*. Madame St Vérain is in the salon and asked me to send you to her as soon as you arrived.'

As she went through the door into the square entrance hall, which had a stone-flagged floor and ancient tapestries hanging on its walls, Elaine felt as always as if she were entering another world; as if the thick stone walls that kept out the heat of the day had also kept out the rush and bustle of modern times.

Turning right, she went through an archway into a corridor the wooden panelling of which had been painted pale blue. Long french windows which opened out into the courtyard gave light into the corridor, which was carpeted. Knowing that Yvan was following her, Elaine went through one of the delicately panelled doors on her left and entered a long room which had three long windows opening on to the stone terrace that ran along the front of this, the longest wing, and overlooked green lawns sweeping down to the glinting river.

A slim graceful woman whose white hair was wound in a chignon on top of her head turned from one of the windows when she heard Elaine enter and came across the room. She was dressed in a simple sleeveless dress of navy blue.

'Ah, Elaine, you are here at last, *chérie,*' she said.

As the thin arms enfolded her Elaine felt tears prick her eyes. Marguerite had always greeted her in this way, warmly and without prejudice. It was something that had never changed.

She was pushed away, held at arm's length while Marguerite's fine eyes, darkly blue like Yvan's, studied her closely.

'How thin you are, and pale!' exclaimed Marguerite. 'So tired-looking, too. But we shall soon change all that with our good food and wine. It is time you came back home, *chérie,* to breathe our clear air and feel the warm sun of Charente. We have missed you.' The dark glance flashed to Yvan, who was standing just behind Elaine with his blazer held over his shoulder. 'You have talked with her?' Marguerite asked him.

'*Oui,* we have talked,' he replied coolly.

'And?' Marguerite's eyes flashed inquisitively from his face to Elaine's and back again.

'And she is as contrary as ever,' he replied mockingly. 'Excuse me, please.' He turned away to leave the room.

'Wait, Yvan,' called his mother. 'Armand would like to see you and Elaine together later. He'll probably be awake about five-thirty. Please remember to come to his room then.'

He nodded and left the room. Marguerite looked round at the shining elegance of its delicate antique furniture and shrugged her shoulders.

'It is a little stiff and formal in here, don't you think, for tea? Let's go into the study.'

Along the corridor they went in the direction of the entrance hall and entered another smaller room. Elaine knew from past experience that it was the most cosy room in the house. Lined with shelves of books and furnished with large leather-covered armchairs, it contained many small personal treasures which Armand St Vérain had collected during his travels in different countries. The sense of having come home was very strong as she glanced around at the dark panelling, the framed watercolours that hung on the walls and had been painted by the artistic Armand in his youth.

She sat down on the tapestry-covered stool where she had always sat and watched a young maid set down a tea-tray on the carved table which Armand had brought back from India. As the girl turned away from the table she glanced at Elaine, a quick, almost furtive glance from soft velvety doe-like eyes.

'Marie, this is Madame Durocher,' said Marguerite crisply, and the girl nodded shyly. 'You know where she is going to sleep, so go up now and unpack her case and hang up her clothing in the closet.'

'Oui, madame.'

The girl left the room. Marguerite lifted the lid of the elegant silver tea-pot, glanced inside the pot and clicked her tongue critically.

'I can only hope she boiled the water,' she commented. 'It's hard to get servants who will live in these days. I took Marie because she is the daughter of one of the vine dressers and is a little backward, you understand. Her memory is like a sieve. I don't think we have had tea since you were here, but I know you like it at this time of the afternoon just as your grandmother did. You still take milk?'

'Yes, please.'

Tea poured in a golden-brown stream from the curving spout of the tea-pot as Marguerite tilted it over a cup.

'Tell me what you have been doing in London,' she said suddenly as if the brief silence irked her.

'I'd much rather you told me about Uncle Armand,' replied Elaine. 'Yvan tells me his condition has improved a little.'

'Ah, *oui,* that is so. He is less depressed. You should have seen his face light up when I read your letter to him saying you were coming and that you hoped for a reconciliation with Yvan. That news made all the difference. You see, he has worried about you—he feels that perhaps he should have stepped in and delayed your marriage, insisted on a long engagement so that you could become accustomed to each other more. He feels that he could have done more to help you adjust to the way of life here in the country. He feels it is his fault that you ran away.'

'Oh, but he shouldn't have worried! It was nothing to do with him,' protested Elaine urgently.

'Then you shall tell him that yourself,' said Marguerite, smiling as she passed the cup and saucer. 'It will relieve his mind even more. I'll take you to see him when you've had your tea and have been to your room to freshen up a little. Yvan will come with us, and when Armand sees you together he'll know that all is forgiven.' Marguerite gave her a sharp searching glance. 'You won't let me down, *chérie,* please? His happiness depends so much on knowing that when he's gone you and Yvan will be here together, bringing up your children. And it's important, isn't it, that a man as gentle and as good as Armand is should die in peace?'

'*Oui,* it is. But Yvan and I aren't...'

'Ah, I know you have your problems in adjusting, you two. *Mon dieu,* what marriage hasn't problems in its early years?' Marguerite went on speaking forcibly, overriding Elaine's objection. 'Especially when the partners come from different backgrounds as you two do. I experienced a little of that myself. My first husband, Jean, was of peasant stock. He always worked close to the land. He was simple in his tastes and habits and was as strong as the rock his family was named after, whereas I was from a *bourgeois* background. My father was a teacher and my mother's family were merchants. Would you like more tea? Another pastry? Eat up, we must put some flesh on your bones. I think you have been starving yourself in London.'

'No, thank you.' Elaine put down her cup. 'Madame ... Aunt Marguerite ... oh, I never know what to call you.'

'I like Tante best, for ever since you were a tiny child coming here with your grandmother I've felt like your aunt. Now what is it you want to tell me?'

'You made a mistake when you read my letter to Uncle Armand.'

'I did?' The dark eyes went wide and the fine white eyebrows arched expressively. 'Was it about the time of your arrival at the airport? The plane was later than I had thought? Is that why you were late arriving here?' Slim long-fingered hands, wrinkled and veined with age yet still graceful in their movements, went up in an expressive gesture, '*Mon dieu,* how I worried when you did not come! The terrible thoughts I had! I thought that perhaps Yvan had drunk too much wine and had crashed the car, that you had been hurt, that I would have to tell Armand that after all you would not be coming to see him and watch the light go from his eyes. But always I worry like that when people are late coming by road.'

'No, it wasn't that. The plane arrived on time. But Yvan wasn't there. We missed each other. I hired a car and drove myself. I was almost here when he caught up with me.'

'Then where is your car? I saw you get out of his when I was looking out from an upstairs window.'

Elaine swallowed. 'There was an accident, a small one. The car went into a ditch.'

'I knew it, I guessed it! You were driving too fast—ah no, don't deny it. You are a madcap. You must always be in a hurry. So that is why you were late!'

'Not really. We stopped to walk in the woods and talk and . . .'

'Ah, yes,' Marguerite was on her feet, 'you would have much to say to each other after all these months apart. I understand. But now you are here and I must go and tell Armand you have come while you go and wash your face and change your dress. You are in the tower suite. Armand is, of course, in the central bedroom in the main wing. I shall see you there in half an hour.'

She went from the room, and left alone Elaine admitted ruefully that she had been very cleverly outmanoeuvred and prevented from telling Marguerite that there was to be no reconciliation between herself and Yvan. Why? For the simple reason that, guessing nothing would please him more than to know that Elaine had been reunited with her husband, Marguerite had lied deliberately to Armand and now she was doing her utmost to make that lie become reality —or at least to appear to be reality.

As she went through to the entrance hall and began to go up the stairs which swept in a curve to the second storey Elaine felt shame flush through her again. In comparison to Marguerite's single-minded devotion to Armand's well-being her own indignant refusal to pretend to be reconciled to Yvan just to ease Armand's mind seemed mean and irresponsible. No wonder Yvan considered her to be selfish. What harm would it do her to pretend to be reconciled? None at all, really, so why bother to insist that Marguerite had made a mistake? Why not go along with Marguerite in her attempts to make Armand's last days happy? It would be a way of proving to Yvan once and for all that she was not selfish or a coward.

Reaching the top of the stairs, she went along a short landing and opened the door of a room. Its wooden panelling was painted pale green and against that background the French colonial-style furniture made from beechwood gleamed golden. On the double bed there was a pretty patchwork quilt, the predominant colours of which were green and gold, and which Elaine guessed had been made by Marguerite herself.

Stepping across to the window, she flung back the shutters which had been closed against the brightness of the sun during the heat of the day. Now it was almost five o'clock and the sun had gone round the corner of the tower so the room was in the shade.

For a moment she lingered at the window to gaze out beyond the courtyard to the cordons of vines she could see on a terraced slope of land. Then she turned into the room and went over to the big cupboard which was built along one wall. The maid Marie had done her work well. The few clothes Elaine had brought were arranged on hangers and below them were her shoes.

On a sudden impulse Elaine opened the other half of the cupboard and felt a flash of irritation. Some of Yvan's clothing hung there, a dark suit, a pair of tough denim working trousers and some shirts. Beneath them were a couple of pairs of shoes and a pair of working boots.

Swinging round, she went over to the tallboy. The top of it was scattered with his belongings; a silver-backed hairbrush; a hand-made wooden box in which he kept odds and ends, such as cuff links, and a half-full packet of cigarettes. Pulling out the top drawer she saw some underwear and socks.

She banged the drawer shut. She had no intention of allowing the pretence at reconciliation go as far as sharing a bedroom with him! That would be too dangerous. As soon as she saw him again she would have to tell him so.

Unzipping her dress, she slipped out of it and hung it in the wardrobe. She found her toilet bag and went through a communicating door into the small bathroom. She washed quickly, sprinkled herself liberally with cologne-scented talc and went back to the bedroom.

She stopped short, just inside the door. when she saw that Yvan was in the bedroom and was in the act of pulling off his shirt over his head. When he was free of it he tossed it into the wicker clothes basket beside the dressing table, and as he turned round gave a start of surprise when he saw her there, dressed only in very brief panties and bra.

'*Eh bien*, this is a surprise,' he drawled. 'Quite a pleasant one,' he added, putting his hands on his hips and surveying her insolently from head to foot. 'I wasn't expecting your company in this room so soon.'

The skin of his wide-shouldered torso was deeply tanned due to the hours he spent out of doors working without a shirt, but where his pants were belted across his flat stomach a line of white skin showed in sharp contrast. His appearance fascinated her as much as her half-dressed state seemed to fascinate him and she had to force herself to look away out of the window, look anywhere in fact than at his tough male beauty.

'Your mother told me to come up here. Jacques had brought my case here and the maid has hung my clothes in the cupboard. I ... I didn't know you still slept here.' Elaine found she was stammering defensively, tightened her lips and lifted her chin and stamped her bare foot on the soft green carpet as she caught his sceptical grin out of the corner of her eyes. 'It's true, I don't want to share a bedroom with you.'

'Then may I suggest you tell my mother that and perhaps she'll arrange for you to have another room,' he replied coolly, and stepping past her he went into the bathroom and closed the door.

For a moment Elaine stood where she was, feeling her flare of anger fade as she realised ruefully that to go to Marguerite and ask to be put in another bedroom would be to admit that no real reconciliation had taken place. On the other hand, if she moved into another bedroom in another part of the house, the rest of the household would also realise that she and Yvan were still separated and in no time the information would seep through to Uncle Armand and all the good which Marguerite was trying to do would be undone.

Frowning over the problem, she stripped quickly

and put on fresh underwear, zipped herself into another dress patterned in brown and white, combed her hair and applied make-up. She was leaning forward watching her reflection in the mirror outline her lips with a deep glossy red when the bathroom door opened and Yvan came back into the room.

'You still here?' he remarked jeeringly as he went over to his side of the wardrobe and opened the doors.

She swung round and leaned back against the dressing table.

'Yvan ... I must tell you ... I've changed my mind,' she began uncertainly.

'Again?' he mocked. 'How you swing to and fro like a weather vane! There's an English nursery rhyme, isn't there, about a girl called Mary who was quite contrary? It could be about you. What have you changed your mind about now? How you feel about me?'

'No, no.' She bit her lower lip hard. She must not allow him to irritate her with his taunts. She must try not to react to them. 'I've decided to agree to your suggestion that we should pretend to be reconciled.'

He had selected a clean shirt, another cream one with a pattern of small blue flowers on it. Holding it in his hand, he turned to look at her with eyes that had narrowed suspiciously.

'So,' he drawled, his mouth twisting with derision, 'the thought of being cut out of his will is too much for you, eh?'

'That has nothing to do with it,' she flared. 'After talking to your mother I've realised that to pretend is for the best. I'm doing it for my uncle's sake and for no other reason, do you hear?'

'*Oui*, I hear,' he murmured as he put an arm into one

sleeve of the shirt. 'Then you'll be staying longer than you had anticipated.'

Elaine hadn't thought of that. In her usual impulsive way she had made a quick decision and hadn't thought of the consequences.

'Only for as long as necessary,' she replied evasively.

'He may linger for weeks, even months,' he said quietly as he buttoned the shirt and pushed the tails into the belted waistband of his trousers. 'Your presence here, his belief that you and I are no longer separated, could give him a new zest for life. I hope you realise that and are willing to pay the price.'

'What price?' she demanded.

He went across to the tallboy, pulled open a drawer and took a tie from it before replying, then came over to stand near her to look in the mirror while he knotted the tie of light blue. Watching the deft movements of his big hands, the tautening of his jaw as he settled the tie under the collar, she was suddenly swamped with memories of other times in this room when she had watched him dress, and she moved away sharply to stand by the window and look out.

'The price of having to pretend to be my loving wife, of course,' Yvan replied mockingly. Now he was brushing his hair and sweeping it back from his forehead. Coal black streaked with ash grey, its controlled shagginess seemed to emphasize and flatter the aquiline distinction of his face rather than detract from it.

'The pretence will only be necessary in front of Uncle Armand,' she said determinedly, and turned away again to look out of the window. Being in this room with him fencing with words about their relationship was doing her nerves no good. Every move he made drew attention to his latent sensuality. She was becoming more and more aware of him on a physical level.

'I disagree,' he said smoothly, as he shrugged into his navy blue blazer and came to stand beside her. 'Jacques is inquisitive and will report everything we do or don't do to Berthe, his wife. The little maid Marie isn't as dumb as she looks either, and her father works in the vineyard. We shall have to be very careful if we don't want Armand suspecting all isn't well. Do you think you can stand the strain of appearing to be my dutiful placid wife for a week or so, possibly a month? Perhaps I should warn you that only in the privacy of this room will you be able to let go and say what you feel about me to my face.' He laughed softly. 'Oh, but I was forgetting. You don't wish to share a room with me. You see, you already create a difficulty by wanting to sleep alone. If only you were a little less of a puritan we could make the most of our so-called reconciliation, enjoy the close contact in which it has placed us.'

While he was speaking he slid an arm round her waist and turned her towards him. His glance slanted to her mouth and as he bent his head she raised her hand to slap his lean cheek. But her hand never made contact because he caught her slender wrist between his fingers and forced her hand down.

'*Mon dieu,* what a temper you have!' he jeered. 'You'll have to control it if we are to make a success of our pretence.'

'Then you'll have to stop tormenting me ... and find another bed to sleep in, won't you?' she countered breathlessly, and managing to wrench her hand free she moved away from him towards the door.

'Now why should I want to torment you? What purpose would it serve?' he queried.

She swung round to face him, the fine pleated skirt of her dress swirling out.

'You're hoping to scare me off. You want me to leave rather than go through with the pretence so that Uncle Armand will cut me out of his will,' she accused. 'You told me, if you remember, that a reconciliation would hardly suit your ends. But I'm not leaving yet. I'm staying for a few days . . . only . . . only I can't sleep with you. Oh, Yvan, please try to understand. I can't do it with someone . . . I don't love.'

For a few seconds of silence he stared at her, and she had the impression that he had gone rather pale. Then he shrugged and turned away to go over and close the bathroom door which he had left open.

'You have some very strange ideas,' he murmured as he came back across the room towards her. 'But it can be arranged for you to sleep alone in this room. I'll sleep in the nursery.'

'The nursery?' she repeated in puzzlement.

'You know, the other room on this floor, where you used to sleep as a child—where, if you had not run away last year, our child might be sleeping soon. That way no one will be any the wiser about our sleeping habits while you're here. Does that suit you?'

Elaine nodded dumbly, once more turning away from him in case he saw the expression on her face. His remark about a child, *their* child, had found an unexpected chink in her armour and had hurt far more than any other of his taunts.

'*Eh bien,* that's settled,' he said practically. 'And now we shall go and see your uncle.' He moved past her to open the door leading to the landing. 'Try to appear less angry with me, *petite,*' he murmured as she walked past him, 'he will guess the truth if you don't. Think why you're doing it—to prevent him from changing his will in my favour. That should give you comfort.'

Armand St Vérain lay in a big four-poster bed facing two long windows that looked over the river. Until the moment she stood beside the bed Elaine had never seen anyone who was seriously ill and dying. When her grandmother had been taken to hospital she had not visited her there because her cousin Charles had not considered the intensive care ward of a London hospital a suitable place for a twelve-year-old child to visit.

So the sight of her great-uncle's emaciated face and hands and the hoarse whisper of his voice shocked her into a sort of numb docility. She found it was impossible not to reassure him that he had not been to blame for her running away.

'And now you are here, you're going to stay with Yvan,' he whispered urgently, raising his head with its sparse white hair from the pillow, staring in her direction with strained, almost blind brown eyes. 'I don't hold with these modern marriages. A wife should be with her husband and a husband should be with his wife. I want to hear you say you'll stay with him and will never run away again.'

Elaine moved uneasily. Across the bed her eyes met those of Marguerite, who was watching her, an expression of appeal on her face. Looking back at her uncle, she said in a low voice,

'I'll stay with Yvan and never run away again, Uncle.'

It had been worth saying, she thought, to see his eyes glimmer with relief, and for a long while she sat with her hand in his, listening to his disjointed ramblings as he recalled past incidents in his life. While she listened she was aware that Yvan had left the room and that only Marguerite was there, sitting at one of the windows, her fingers busy with some quilting as she watched the sun sliding down to the horizon and the shadows lengthening over the land.

At last Armand fell asleep. Elaine removed her hand from his lax hold and with Marguerite she left the room, handing over the care of the old man to a nurse who would stay with him through the night. They went downstairs to the dining room where candles in silver candelabra glinted on the cutlery and white linen of the dinner table.

Yvan joined them at the table and they ate a local dish of goose cooked with onions, garlic and tomatoes which was followed by one of Elaine's favourite desserts, a lemon delight, smooth and tangy, which melted in the mouth. One of the white wines produced in the area accompanied the food which was served by Jacques and, although she had not felt hungry when she had sat down at the table, Elaine ate well and drank two glasses of wine.

All through the meal Marguerite kept a conversation going, confining it mostly to the weather and Armand's health. Yvan said little, but then he had never indulged much in small talk at the meal table, thought Elaine, glancing at him covertly and comparing him with his vivacious mother. He must take after his father more than Marguerite, she decided. Only the colour of his eyes, the fine chiselling of his features and the grace of his long-fingered hands were like Marguerite's.

When the meal was over Marguerite excused herself, saying she felt very tired and intended to go to bed to rest in case Armand should need her in the night.

'Your coming, although it has relieved him in some

ways, has also excited him,' she said to Elaine, 'and I fear he might have a restless night.'

'Can I do anything to help?' offered Elaine, noting that fatigue and worry had aged Marguerite very much during the past few months. Suffering and sadness had laid their marks on the fine-featured face and covered the soft skin with a network of tiny wrinkles.

'Not tonight, *chérie*.' Marguerite's hand pressed on her shoulder affectionately. 'Tonight you must rest also, for you have driven a long way. *Et maintenant*, I wish you goodnight. Jacques will serve coffee for you in the study.'

In the smoke-scented study Elaine was pouring the coffee into tiny porcelain cups when the telephone on the desk rang. The sound of it reminded her that she had promised to phone Gerald Morton and tell him that she had arrived safely. She would also have to tell him that she would be staying longer than she had expected. Sipping her coffee, hearing Yvan's deep voice speaking rapidly to whoever was on the other end of the line, she wondered what Gerald would think when she told him that her return to London was delayed.

Would he think she was procrastinating again? For several weeks he had been urging her to find a way to put an end to her marriage. When she had gone to ask him if she could have a day off to enable her to come to Chambourtin he had said:

'Now is your chance to be rid of Durocher! You're bound to see him and it will be much easier to make him see the reality of the situation when you're face to face with him.'

'No, it won't be any easier,' she had disagreed. 'You don't know him. He ... he's very inflexible, and we were married in church and I doubt very much if he believes in divorce.'

'In this day and age?' Gerald's hazel eyes had expressed his scorn. 'Oh, come off it, Elaine. It happens all the time. You should be able to plead incompatibility, surely. Why you ever fell for him in the first place I'll never understand. He must be years older than you are, besides being a foreigner.' He had given her an assessing glance. 'I suppose it was the old story. You fell for his Gallic charm. Heady stuff when it's used against a romantic background of an old chateau set among vineyards and roses, I should think.'

'He's exactly twelve years older than I am, just as you are,' Elaine had snapped rather haughtily. 'And you seem to forget that I'm a little bit French myself, so I don't think of my relatives and friends at Chambourtin as foreigners.'

He had stared at her, his eyebrows raised in surprise for a moment, then he said equably,

'I was only trying to point out to you where there might be incompatibility. You can't go on like this for ever, you know, married to him yet living apart from him. You might want to marry someone else.'

She had been a little perturbed then, and wondered if he was going to ask her to marry him, not knowing how to answer him.

'I suppose so,' she had muttered. 'I'll be back as soon as I can, but if it looks as if I might have to stay longer to be with my uncle I'll let you know.'

He had merely nodded, and she had left his office feeling a little as if she had said goodbye to him for good.

'Would you like some cognac with your coffee?' Yvan's voice interrupted the flow of her thoughts and brought her back from the cold businesslike atmosphere of Gerald's office to the soft light and shadows of the study. Yvan was offering her a delicate glass goblet in which the liquid gold produced by the Charente sunshine glimmered. She took the glass from him and sipped some of the heart-warming liqueur, hoping to gain some courage from it.

He poured brandy for himself and sat down in one of the deep leather armchairs. Light from a nearby lamp illuminated the clean-cut angles of his face and the darkly bright gleam of his eyes.

'May I use the phone?' she asked.

'*Oui,* I suppose you can.' He replaced his coffee cup on its saucer and picked up his brandy glass again, cupping it in his hands to warm it and raising it to his nostrils to sniff the aroma.

'It'll be a long-distance call, person to person. I . . . er . . . promised someone I'd phone to say I had arrived safely here,' she explained.

'Someone?' he queried, and across the rim of the goblet his eyes glinted wickedly through their thick lashes. 'Your cousin Charles or his wife Jenny, perhaps? Do you know their number by heart? If you don't, it's there in the small book beside the phone. It'll be necessary, of course, for you to get the assistance of the operator.'

Elaine glanced sideways at the gilt and white telephone. She couldn't possibly talk to Gerald in front of Yvan. Even though she would be speaking in English Yvan would understand most of what she would be saying and he had enough intelligence to guess at anything which he couldn't understand.

'Is there another phone I could use?' she asked.

'An extension, you mean? Only in my mother's room and in the kitchen. But please, do go ahead and use this one.'

She made no move to the desk. She sipped some more brandy and poured more coffee for herself, wondering how long she would have to wait for him to realise that she wished to be alone when she made the call. Several times she glanced at him where he sat at ease, apparently absorbed in a book he had taken from one of the shelves, and occasionally lifting his glass to sip brandy.

'More coffee?' she offered at last in desperation.

'Hmm?' he did not look up.

'I asked you if you'd like more coffee.'

'Non, merci.' He placed his empty goblet on the side table, closed the book and put it aside too, then forward with his arms crossed on his knees. 'This is pleasant, isn't it—quite like old times sitting here together,' he murmured.

It wasn't like old times at all and he knew it, she thought furiously, watching his mouth curve ironically. In the first four months of their marriage they had never reached this stage. They had never sat alone in this room. When they had been alone together they had never sat apart or silent. They had always sat close to each other, either on the terrace under the stars when the weather had been warm, or when it had been cool or wet they had sat in the shadows of the salon. But never had they sat in silence and never for long, preferring to go to their bedroom in the tower, to lie close to each other on the bed and make love.

'Have you made your phone call?' he asked politely.

'Oh, you know I haven't!' she flared. 'I can't make it with you sitting there listening to every word I say.'

'I see. Then it isn't to Charles or Jenny you make the call. The someone is a friend?' The dark eyes seemed to bore into hers as if he were trying to X-ray her mind and see what was hiding in it. 'Another man with whom you are having an extra-marital affair, perhaps?' he drawled.

Indignation flared up in Elaine and she couldn't contain it any longer. Springing to her feet, she glared down at his sardonically smiling face, her fingers working at her sides as they itched to slap him.

'Unlike you ...' she began, caught her breath shakily and continued in a low furious whisper. 'Unlike you, I don't go in for extra-marital affairs. And since you haven't the manners to leave the room while I make the call I'll write a letter instead. Good night!'

She stalked from the room, banging the door shut behind her, and rushed through the dim echoing entrance hall up the curving staircase to the bedroom.

The sight of Yvan's hairbrush on the dressing table where he had tossed it down annoyed her further, and on sudden impulse she crossed the room, opened the wardrobe and began to take his clothes from it. With a pile of them over one arm she went along the passage to the other bedroom, opened the door and switched on the light, then stared with dismay at the small child's bed where once she had slept. Yvan would never be able to sleep on it in any comfort! He was too big.

Oh well, it had been his decision to sleep in here, so he could put up with it. Going over to the small wardrobe, she hung his suit in it and went back for more of his belongings. It took her four trips, but at last she had removed everything. For a moment she stood in the little room looking at the pretty curtains, at the few books of fairy tales which had once belonged to her grandmother and which had been passed on to herself, at the battered hobbyhorse which still leaned in a corner. She felt nostalgia sweep over her for the happy carefree childish summers she had spent here, walking and talking with her great-uncle, listening to his stories of the days of chivalry when knights in armour had ridden about Aquitaine and the Duchess Eleanor had held the last court of love in Poitiers.

But her childhood was over, and so was the Age of Chivalry. With a sigh Elaine switched out the light and closed the door and returned to the other room. Sitting down at the small writing table, she took out pen and paper and began to write a letter to Gerald.

Ten minutes later she gave up trying to write. Indignation caused by Yvan's behaviour was still bubbling up, making it impossible for her to explain in cool clear sentences, which wouldn't betray the state of tumult her emotions were in, exactly why she would have to stay at Chambourtin longer than she had expected.

Tiredness was washing over her in waves, so after undressing and slipping into a thin cotton nightgown she climbed into bed and fell asleep almost immediately.

CHAPTER THREE

ELAINE woke early next morning and knew without opening her eyes where she was by the sound of doves cooing as they sat on the curving eaves of the pointed roof of the tower.

For a brief moment of elation her mind played a trick on her. The nine months of separation from Yvan were wiped out as if they had never been and she believed she was only four months married and still very much in love. Eyes still closed, she smiled, a sensual movement of her soft lips, stretched her legs languorously and rolled over on to her side, her arm reaching out to encircle ... *nothing*!

The feel of cool empty sheets shocked her back into the present. She opened her eyes and stared at the curve of the pillow which had not been touched by a head. She was alone and had been alone all night.

Squeezing her eyes shut against the painful surge of disappointment that swept over her, she lay on her stomach wishing she could forget the sudden gnawing ache of physical frustration in the oblivion of sleep. How was she going to put in days, possibly weeks, of living in the same house as Yvan and remain emotionally and physically aloof from him? How could she waken in this bed without remembering other awakenings when he had been there beside her, warm and relaxed, his arm about her trapping her in the prison created by her love for him?

If only she could be indifferent to him! If only the sight and sound of him did not produce this awful nagging feeling of regret because the love that they had both sworn would last until death parted them had, apparently, never existed.

If he had loved her, surely he would never have done what Solange Bourget had claimed he had done. Surely he would never have stayed the night with Solange in her apartment in Angoulême—not only once but on several occasions when he had been supposedly in Cognac on business.

An image of Solange flashed on to the screen of Elaine's imagination. Tall and slender with great dark eyes in a thin sallow face framed by long black hair, Solange was an artist. She was the same age as Yvan and had known him for years, ever since adolescence. She had been passing by Chambourtin, so she had said, returning from a year's stay in the Caribbean where she had been painting, and had called in a week or so after Elaine and Yvan had been married to see her old sweetheart, as she had called him.

She had obviously been surprised to find he was married and had teased him about it. She herself had never married, she had confided to Elaine, because she liked her freedom too much; and anyway, why should anyone bother to get married unless it was for convenience, possibly to raise a family, or when some material advantage such as property or wealth could be gained?

As soon as Solange left Chambourtin after that short visit Elaine had forgotten her. She had been too caught up in the happiness of being married to Yvan, because they had been very happy, to spare a thought for another woman in his life, and on the few occasions he was away from her it had never entered her head to suspect he might be lying to her or doing something different from what he had told her he would be doing.

Then one cold damp day in early November, when it seemed that the wind that made the russet leaves dance about had swept straight in from the grey wastes of the Atlantic Ocean, which lay to the west beyond the marshes, Elaine went shopping in Angoulême, that cathedral town so splendidly set on a promontory above the Charente river.

Because she found the wind chilly she had stepped inside the delightful old house near the cathedral which had once been a Bishop's palace but had been turned into a museum, and she had come face to face with Solange.

The woman had greeted her pleasantly and after a brief conversation about the collection of African sculpture which was on show, she had invited Elaine to her studio apartment nearby. Impressed by Solange's unconventional attitude to life and a little overawed by her success as an artist, Elaine had been flattered by the invitation and had gone to the old house where Solange rented the top floor, which had a view over the tangled towers and twisted streets of the old town.

During the next three weeks the visit to the studio had been repeated; and now Elaine moved restlessly in bed, groaning a little at her own innocence and gullibility and wishing she had never let herself be charmed into visiting Solange. If she hadn't gone to the studio she would never have had her distrust of Yvan aroused, for no matter how often each visit had begun with a general discussion it had always ended with Yvan: about how fond Solange had been of him when they were younger; about how they had often gone away for weekends together, and all the time

Solange had implied that the relationship had been anything but innocent.

'Oh, I knew I wasn't the only girl he took about. There were others,' Solange had shrugged. 'But he always came back to me. Even now he's married...' She had broken off and put up a thin hand to lift the heavy fringe of straight black hair back from her forehead. '*Mon dieu,*' she whispered, 'what am I saying? Always I forget.'

'Forget what?' Elaine asked.

'That you're his wife. You're so young and innocent that it's hard to imagine you with Yvan, who is tough and experienced. I can imagine you better with someone young like yourself, a nice fresh boy, an English boy with blue eyes and fair hair. *Oui*, I can imagine you holding hands, laughing a little self-consciously when you kiss. Ah, Elaine, why did you marry Yvan?'

'Because I love him, of course,' Elaine replied simply, although she had been strangely disturbed by Solange's word picture.

An odd gleam came into Solange's dark eyes, a sort of mocking pity.

'But of course. You are a romantic and believe in love, and you believe he married you for the same reason. But you should know that in the life of this province, until half a century ago, marriage in the *bourgeois* and upper classes was a matter for arrangement or for convenience. Love existed only outside the arrangement, unless of course the partners were lucky and learned to love each other. Nowadays there is more chance of lovers marrying, but in the case of Yvan,' Solange made a grimace and shrugged, 'ah, he isn't the son of Marguerite Durocher for nothing.'

'I'm afraid I don't understand,' Elaine whispered in bewilderment.

'She was prevented from marrying Armand St Vérain. She wasn't considered good enough, you see, to be his wife, so she did the next best thing. She married Jean Durocher, a man of great strength, charm and shrewdness; an ambitious man who was employed by Armand St Vérain to oversee the cultivation of the great vineyards of Chambourtin.' Solange reached for a cigarette and lit it to inhale its smoke before she went on with a shrug, 'Oh, it was well known in this area that Marguerite married him for convenience so that she could live near Armand and see him practically every day, and eventually she achieved her ambition to become the chatelaine of the famous chateau when her husband died and she was able to marry Armand.'

'But just because she married for convenience it doesn't mean to say Yvan has married *me* for convenience,' Elaine protested. 'People don't do that any more.'

Solange's glance once again gleamed with mocking pity.

'How naïve you are,' she drawled. 'Yvan must have found it very easy to seduce you. I suppose all he had to do was to kiss you a few times and caress your body for you to believe he loved you. Like many other silly little girls you confused physical passion with love.'

Elaine had been too shocked and shaken by Solange's forthrightness to make any immediate reply, but at last she had managed to make another feeble protest.

'But what could he gain from marrying me? I've no fortune, no property.'

'Not yet perhaps, but one day you will have. You're the only person surviving with any St Vérain blood who has any sort of hereditary claim to Chambourtin.

Presumably when Armand dies you'll inherit it. I wouldn't be surprised if Marguerite knew that and arranged for Yvan to marry you herself. She would talk Armand into it by suggesting that it would be a good idea if he, who had become his stepson, the only sort of son he was likely to have, could share Chambourtin with you.'

'Oh, this is absolutely ridiculous! Wherever did you get such an idea?' Elaine demanded.

'Where do you think?' retorted Solange. 'From Yvan himself, your husband, *ma chère*. He married you on condition that Armand changed his will and made him co-heir with you to Chambourtin.'

'I don't believe you! Yvan married me for love, I know he did.' Elaine's protestation was frantic.

'Did he? Then ask him why he comes here to see me. Ask him why he has stayed here several nights with me since I returned. Ask him why he was here last night, when he left those behind him,' Solange demanded, her dark eyes glittering with malice as she pointed to a small table. On it had been a pair of leather driving gloves and a cigarette lighter which Elaine recognised at once as belonging to Yvan.

'Do you still think he married you for love?' Solange queried softly. 'I know he didn't. I know he is a cool, practical schemer like his mother. He has looked ahead and agreed to an arranged marriage to better himself. As for love, he loves me, always has done and always will...'

Elaine hadn't stayed to hear any more. She had run from the studio high above the roof-tops of the town and had clattered down the stairs to the busy street. The tall twin towers of the cathedral had loomed over her as she scrambled into her uncle's car, which she'd borrowed to drive into Angoulême.

Seated behind the steering wheel she had tried very hard to control the trembling which had seized her as a result of the shock Solange had inflicted upon her, But it had taken longer than she thought, and by the time she had been able to drive darkness had come down and light had been twinkling from the buildings.

Feeling lonelier than she had ever thought it was possible to feel, she left the city and drove north. Somewhere along the Route Nationale she decided she could not go back to Chambourtin, so she had driven straight past the end of the road which led to it and had gone on to Poitiers, arriving there, cold and exhausted, late at night. She had taken a room at a small hotel where she had spent a sleepless night, unable to cope with the raw pain which had slashed through her when she saw Yvan's gloves and lighter in Solange's apartment.

Next morning she had driven to the station, parked the car and caught the train to Paris. From the safety of that distance she had phoned the chateau; Jacques had answered the call and she had told him to pass on a message to Yvan when he returned from Cognac where he had supposedly been attending the annual wine growers' conference. Jacques was to tell him she had gone back to England to visit her cousins and would be writing to him.

On arriving in London she had not gone to Ashleigh, where her cousins lived, but had stayed with an old school friend for a few days. She would have liked to have remained in the seclusion of her friend's flat indefinitely, only her friend became worried about her and contacted Charles and Jenny, with the result that Jenny had arrived one afternoon and had taken Elaine down to Ashleigh.

They had been very good to her, Elaine realised that now. They had passed no comment when she had told them she had left Yvan and had no intention of returning to him. Charles had found her another job as a secretarial assistant in the wine-importing offices where she had come in contact with Gerald Morton again.

She had written to Yvan telling him she realised she had made a mistake in marrying him in such a hurry, and that she needed time to think about their relationship. In answer a letter had come from her uncle imploring her to return to her husband. Nothing had come from Yvan until March, when he had written:

'You have had time to think. Please let me know when you're coming back.'

The cool arrogance of the letter had reopened the wound. If he had come to London and had pleaded with her to return to him; if he had said in the letter that he loved her and wanted her back she would have gone. But he had remained aloof, and she had seen in his coolness a lack of feeling that finally convinced her that he hadn't married her for love. So she had replied saying that she had decided to stay in London, and that eventually she hoped arrangements could be made for them to be divorced. He had not answered the letter.

Elaine turned on to her back and looked at the ceiling. Now she was back at the place she had vowed she would never come back to, and everyone believed she had returned to live with Yvan. Only he and she knew the truth. She was caught in a dangerous pretence and . . .

There was a knock on the door. It was pushed open slightly and Yvan looked round the edge of it. At the sight of him she sat up quickly and defensively.

'May I come in?' he asked.

'Oui.'

He entered and closed the door behind him. Seeing his dark gaze flick over her she wished she hadn't sat up in such a hurry, because the bedclothes had fallen away from her, revealing the fact that one of the straps of her nightgown had slipped off a shoulder and as a result the bodice was sagging down to expose one creamy rounded breast. With an effort to appear nonchalant she pulled the strap up, hunched her knees under the bedclothes and leaned forward to hug them with her arms.

'What do you want?' she asked.

'My boots,' he replied, coming into the room to stand at the foot of the bed and stare at her from under frowning eyebrows. He was dressed in his working denims and the tight fit of the faded blue shirt emphasized his muscular physique handed down to him from his peasant forebears. 'I have to thank you for moving my clothes into the other room. Unfortunately you didn't move my shoes or boots. Please excuse me while I get them.'

His politeness was freezing. It chilled Elaine to the marrow, making her shiver although the room was warm.

'Of course,' she murmured.

Yvan went round the end of the bed to the wardrobe, opened it and took out the boots. Then to her consternation he sat on the edge of the bed quite close to her. Furtively she tried to slide across to the other side of the bed, only to find that the skirt of her nightgown was trapped under the bedclothes beneath his weight.

'Did you sleep well?' he asked politely as he pulled one boot on.

'Yes, thank you. Did you?' she said stiffly.

'I've slept better,' he replied curtly, and tugged on the other boot. She glanced at his face. It was taut and dark, scored with lines of weariness, and she remembered with a prick of conscience the smallness of the bed in the nursery.

'I'm sorry,' she said impulsively, 'that bed can't be very comfortable for you. It's too small and narrow.'

'Possibly,' he said, and stood up, much to her secret relief. He walked over to the window, pulled it open and thrust back the shutters. At once sunlight streamed into the room. 'I didn't sleep in it, so I don't know,' he added.

'Then where did you sleep?' she exclaimed without thinking. Yvan was leaning against the window frame looking down at something in the courtyard. The sunshine gilded his face, so that for a moment it looked like a mask of gold. Then he smiled slightly, turned to glance at her and the image was destroyed.

'I'll let you guess where,' he retorted softly, provocatively, and at once her mind became busy with all sorts of conjectures.

'Perhaps it would be best if I slept in the other room,' she said coolly.

'That would be one solution to the problem, but not the best one, in my opinion,' he said, and lunging away from the window frame he began to stride towards the door. His hip caught against the writing table and the letter which she had begun to write to Gerald fluttered to the floor. He bent to pick it up, glanced at it and raised his eyebrows.

' "Dear Gerald," ' he read in English, exaggerating his French accent so that he sounded as if he hadn't had any instruction in the language at all. ' "*H*as you will see, I arrive 'ere today. I 'ave seen my uncle and 'e-

wishes me to stay near 'im for a while."'

Thrusting back the bedclothes, Elaine leapt from the bed and bounded to his side, hand reaching to snatch the letter from him.

'How dare you read my letter!' she seethed.

Her hand never touched the paper because he raised it above his head and waved it tauntingly. As she failed to reach her objective she fell against him, unable to stop the momentum of her fast-moving body. At once his other arm closed about her and once again she found herself held close against him.

'Let me go!' she cried, writhing in that vice-like hold, 'and give me my letter!'

'Only if you tell me about this Gerald,' he taunted.

'Yvan, you're hurting me,' she gasped.

'No, I'm not. If you didn't struggle so much against me you wouldn't get hurt. You'll always be hurt by your own impetuosity, *chérie. Stay still.*'

He uttered the last words so forcibly and tightened his hold on her so mercilessly that she stopped twisting to stand with her head down, her breast rising and falling as she tried to recover her breath.

'Is he your lover?' he demanded.

'Why should I tell you?' she countered, flinging back her hair and glaring up at him.

'I have a right to know.'

'Oh, you and your rights,' she said scathingly. 'I have rights too, the right to know where you slept last night, but you didn't tell me.'

'I slept on the sofa in the study.'

His equable answer disconcerted her. She leaned back against the iron-like bar of his arm and stared at him, studying his eyes to try to read their expression. They met hers steadily, deeply indigo under their heavy lids. Her glance drifted down to his mouth and saw the firm lips curve slightly, sardonically.

'I don't believe you,' she said.

'*Zut*,' he rasped angrily. 'Then I'll try again. I slept in the bed of another woman. I'm sure you'll believe that! Now about this Gerald. Is he the reason why you've come here talking about divorce?'

Elaine put her hands against his chest and tried to push free, only to find he was now holding her with both arms, having dropped her letter to the floor.

'Oh, I can't possibly discuss that with you while you're holding me like this,' she evaded.

'Then how would you like me to hold you? Like this?' he murmured, and slid one of his arms up her back so that his hand could curve round the nape of her neck while his other hand slipped downwards in a provocative intimate caress over the small of her back, at the same time pressing her closer to him so that through the thin cotton of her nightgown she felt the thrust of his thighs and hips against hers.

Desire leapt within her, sending her senses spinning out of control. Hardly knowing what she was doing she leaned against him, instinctively lifting her mouth for his kiss, seeing from beneath her lowered lashes his mouth hover tormentingly above hers. Impatient because by now her whole body was clamouring to be taken, she moved her lips, parting them slightly, invitingly. His mouth came nearer and touched hers fleetingly, and the feel of it was warm and agonisingly familiar. With a little groan she lifted her arms to encircle his neck and pressed herself even closer against him.

The door behind them opened. A voice spoke gaspingly.

'Oh, *excusez-moi. madame, monsieur.*'

Yvan's arms fell to his sides and he stepped back. A

little unsteadily Elaine turned, pushing her hair back from her neck with both hands. In the doorway was Marie, the young maid. Her pale cheeks were flushed a dusky pink and her velvety eyes were darting this way and that.

'What is it, Marie?' Yvan spoke gently as he moved past Elaine. Under his feet the fallen letter crackled as he stepped on it.

'I . . . I . . .' The girl was trembling as with shock and seemed incapable of speech. Abruptly she turned and darted out of the doorway and reappeared holding a tray in a rather wobbly fashion. On the tray was a small wicker bread basket, a dish of conserve and a bowl of steaming chocolate. '*Pour madame,*' croaked Marie.

'*Merci,* Marie. Thank you very much,' said Elaine, making an effort and going forward to take the tray from the trembling girl. Marie bobbed her head, whirled and fled.

Yvan looked down at the tray, his glance going over the embroidered linen cloth, the basket of fresh croissants and the steaming chocolate. His mouth curved.

'Breakfast in bed, hmm? It seems there's someone in this house who wants you to stay,' he commented, and turning on his heel he went from the room and closed the door behind him.

Elaine carried the tray over to the bedside table and then sat down on the side of the bed. Face in her hands, elbows on her knees, she struggled to calm herself. Gradually the tumult of her emotions subsided and she was able to lift the bowl of chocolate and drink from it. The delicious creamy sweetness of it reminded her of other breakfasts she had taken in this room.

As she set the bowl down she noticed the red rose for the first time. Freshly picked from the garden, its velvety petals were only just unfurled, and for her its delicate yet heady scent was the essence of Chambourtin. It had been placed in a slim glass vase and its presence on the tray was an expression of welcome.

It seems there is someone in this house who wants you to stay. Yvan's words echoed through Elaine's mind. That someone, she guessed, was Marguerite, who had probably instructed that a breakfast tray should be sent up, spoiling her in the way that she had always spoiled her when she had stayed at the chateau for those long summer holidays as a child.

But Yvan didn't want her to stay—she was becoming more and more sure of that. He was going out of his way to torment her into leaving. Look how he had just behaved, taunting her about her letter to Gerald. She jumped to her feet and moved about the room restlessly, thinking of how he had almost kissed her but not quite.

How could she have behaved with such abandon—inviting him to kiss her, more or less inviting him to take her? How he must be laughing at her! Only yesterday she had told him that she couldn't sleep with someone she didn't love, yet just now he had only to hold her in his arms for her to become a mass of throbbing desire. If Marie hadn't opened the door just then ... oh, it didn't bear thinking about, but she must try to avoid a recurrence of such a situation.

Returning to the tray, she broke open a *croissant*, smothered it with orange conserve and crammed it into her mouth. The taste of it gave her an appetite for more and soon she had eaten all four *croissants* and was licking conserve from her fingers.

There were so many things about living at Chambourtin that she loved, she thought as she leaned forward to sniff the fragrance of the rose. She loved the sunshine, the roses, the wine, and she had missed them all these past nine months and wondered vaguely how she could have stayed away so long.

With a sudden lift of spirits, she set off for the bathroom and saw her crumpled letter lying on the floor. She picked it up and on sudden impulse ripped it across. There was no hurry. She could write later, and as she watched the torn pieces of paper whirl down into the waste basket she laughed suddenly, recognising at once the influence of Chambourtin. There was no hurry here, just the slow majestic pace of one day of sunlight following another, slowly ripening the vines.

Half an hour later, dressed in thin cotton slacks and a sleeveless cotton shirt, her hair tied back in a ponytail, Elaine went downstairs and carried the tray into the kitchen. Marguerite was there, seated at the table writing out a menu.

'*Bonjour*, Elaine. How are you?' she said.

'Very well, thank you. And you?'

'Not bad.' Marguerite's shrug was expressive. Elaine gave her a closer look and saw that her face too was lined with weariness.

'How is Uncle this morning?' she asked. 'Did he have a good night?'

'No, he was very restless. He woke up and insisted on speaking to Yvan. Fortunately Yvan hadn't gone to bed.' Marguerite frowned and looked up searchingly. 'I am sorry, *chérie*, that your first night home should have been disturbed to such an extent. It was almost four this morning before Yvan was able to leave Armand's bedside.'

Elaine's lips compressed as she controlled a desire to blurt out that she hadn't known Yvan had sat up most of the night with her uncle. She stared down at the tray which she had placed on the table, not seeing the empty bowl and basket but seeing instead Yvan's face, taut with weariness. Why hadn't he told her what he had been doing all night? Why had he let her think he had gone somewhere else to sleep? Why did he prevaricate when she questioned him—was it to torment her? Or was it because he didn't want her to know what sort of a person he was?

'I wasn't disturbed,' she said, 'but I didn't know he'd sat with my uncle. He didn't tell me.'

'And so you assume that he isn't capable of such a generous act. Is that it?' Marguerite's voice was sharp and her glance was accusing. 'But Yvan is a good man, as his father was before him. And I wish always that he could be happy.'

'Isn't he happy?' asked Elaine.

'I don't think so. Oh, he doesn't go around saying he isn't happy, he's never been one to put his true feelings on show for all the world to see. But I have noticed that he is sometimes, how we say in French, *distrait*, and sometimes he drinks too much, and I have been inclined to blame you.'

'Me?' Elaine squeaked.

'Yes. You haven't been a good wife to him and I wonder sometimes if he regrets having married you.'

Elaine quivered where she stood. There was only one reason why Yvan might have regretted being married to her as far as she knew; he might have preferred to marry Solange. For a moment as she met Marguerite's inquisitive gaze she was tempted to tell her that she knew about Yvan's association with Solange, that she was quite willing to go through with a divorce because she had found him to be far from the perfect husband.

Then she remembered that she and Yvan were supposed to be reconciled, and realised suddenly that

Marguerite had merely been stating her own traditionalist view of marriage. It was a wife's job to make her husband happy and to bear and look after any children which resulted from the marriage. Never in a hundred years would Marguerite understand her own more contemporary attitude, that just because a woman became a wife it did not mean she should sacrifice her right to be an individual.

'I enjoyed my breakfast,' she said, and picked up the tray again, not wishing to offend Marguerite by arguing with her. 'You must have shown Marie how to set the tray.'

'*Oui,* but I said nothing about putting a red rose on it,' replied Marguerite coolly. 'Put the tray by the sink. Marie will attend to it later. Now what would you like to do today?'

But Elaine wasn't listening. She was staring at the tray again as she carried it over to the sink. If neither Marie nor Marguerite had put the rose on the tray, who had? She put the tray down, took the rose from the vase and tucked its long stem through a buttonhole where her blouse fastened at the cleavage between her breasts.

'I asked what would you like to do today?' Marguerite's voice had lost its sharpness and sounded amused. Elaine started and looked round.

'I'd like to help. Can I sit with Uncle Armand?'

'Perhaps later. I expect he'll ask to see you. Why don't you go outside this morning and walk round the garden before the sun gets too hot?'

Elaine did not need to be told twice. Leaving the kitchen, she stepped into the courtyard. Bees were droning among the flowers and the scent of wine casks and roses was as strong as ever. As she passed by the lily pond a gaggle of geese, their fine white feathers glistening in the sunshine, waddled away from her, honking furiously and occasionally turning their long necks to hiss at her.

As she walked through the archway between two *chais* Elaine shaded her eyes against the sun's rays and looked across the undulating land dipping down to a bend of the river. Long lines of vines made the land look as if it were ribbed. Here and there she could see the dark figure of a worker moving along between two rows bending to nip off unnecessary shoots which appeared, overnight, so it seemed, between the main branches of the vines and which had to be kept under control if the plants were to bear good quality grapes.

The gleam of the river beckoned to her and soon she was walking down a stony path which arrowed straight between the vines to the line of willows and aspens which edged the river bank.

The path ended at a wooden jetty to which two old-fashioned punt-like boats were tied up. Flat-bottomed and shallow, they had once been used to convey farm produce and even cattle from the estate to the nearest market town. But for Elaine they had always provided a means of escape. Delighted to find them there, she stepped into one of them, untied it from the jetty and let it drift slowly away from the land while she looked for the long wooden pole she intended to use to push the boat along through the water and which should have been in the bottom of the boat.

For a moment surprise held her still. She blinked and looked again. No, her first glance had not deceived her. There was no pole in the bottom of the boat.

Berating herself silently for being a forgetful fool and untying the boat without making sure first that it was prepared, she looked round quickly, thinking she might be able to leap back on to the jetty. But while she had been looking for the pole the boat had been sidling slowly downstream, pushed along by a current the strength of which wasn't obvious on the smooth shining surface of the water, and now the distance between it and the jetty was far too wide for her to jump across.

Raising her hands to her mouth, Elaine cupped them and shouted, hoping to attract the attention of one of the corkers in the vineyard. Then she waved both arms above her head. No one looked up as the punt slid past the shore and was hidden by a screen of tall poplars from the sight of anyone who might be looking from the land.

Slowly, silently, she was being carried away between the green banks which were too distant for her to reach except by swimming. Since the weather was calm and warm she wasn't really worried. She lay down in the bottom of the boat, pillowing her head on her hands to gaze up at the cloudless blue sky, hearing the occasional gurgle of the water against the side of the boat.

She was the Lady of Shalott whom she had read about in a poem at school, she thought fancifully, being borne along the river to many-towered Camelot because she had made the mistake of looking directly at bold Sir Lancelot. Only the lady in the poem had been dead, and she was very much alive and really ought to be doing something to guide the boat in to the shore somehow.

Sitting up, she saw that the boat was now in a much wider part of the river, a straight part where the water flowed faster between the green selvage of the banks. Leaning over one side, she tried to paddle with one hand, pushing the water backwards as hard as she could, hoping to turn the front of the boat towards one of the banks. But the boat was too heavy and didn't respond at all to her efforts. it was useless too for her to try and row the boat using her two hands, because when she sat in the middle of the boat she was too far from each side to reach over into the water.

Elaine tried to remember what the river was like further along. It grew wider, she knew, and somewhere there was a weir, quite a steep fall of water from one level to another. When she tipped her head to one side she was sure she could hear, above the soft lapping of water against the idle boat and the rustle of reeds on the banks, a subdued roar of water falling.

Panic gripped her suddenly. She stood up and measured with a glance the distance to the nearest bank, kicked off her low-heeled sandals and rolled up the flared legs of her pants. She stood for a precarious moment on the gunwale of the boat, then launched herself forward to dive into the shimmering green-dappled water.

Warm water, rank with the smell of weed, closed over her head. She surfaced, shook her hair which had lost its confining ribbon, and struck out in a slow easy crawl for the bank.

The distance which she had to swim wasn't far, about the length of a normal-sized swimming pool, and although she felt the under-surface current pulling at her she was a sufficiently strong swimmer to resist its sideways tug. Soon her knees struck the bottom of the river and she was able to stand up and wade through the long reeds that grew in the muddy shallows.

She sat on the sloping grassy bank and put her head between her knees, catching her breath. After a while her heart stopped pounding and she looked up. The punt had gone, carried round the bend in the river.

Standing up, Elaine wrung the water out of her hair and shook it back, laughing a little to herself about her escapade. What a thing to happen on her first day home, and how like her to get into such a situation!

'I'm glad you can laugh about it,' said a familiar voice behind her, and she whirled to find Yvan standing astride a bicycle which he had presumably ridden along the towpath.

'Where did you come from?' she gasped.

'I'm on my way back from looking at the vineyard near the river loop. First I see an empty boat drift by, then I come across you. What were you trying to do, drown yourself?'

'No, there was no pole in the punt and I didn't find out until after I'd cast off. I couldn't stop it or make it change course, so I swam to the shore. Anyway, I doubt if anyone could drown in that river. It isn't very deep and the current is sluggish.'

'My father drowned in it,' he said quietly.

That shocked her.

'Oh, I didn't know . . .' she began.

'There's a lot you don't know,' he jeered. 'And when you don't know something, instead of asking about it and finding out in the proper way you make wild guesses and believe they're the truth.'

'Oh, that isn't fair!' she protested, surprised at his sudden attack. 'I didn't know about your father because you didn't tell me about him. You've never told me anything.'

'Because you never cared enough to ask,' he retorted.

'I did care,' she cried out.

'But not enough to come and ask me if what Solange had told you was true or not. Not enough to give me a chance to explain,' he replied roughly. 'Everyone has a right to be given a fair hearing, but you didn't allow me mine. *Mais non,* when you found out something about me that you didn't like, something which touched your self-esteem, you behaved like the spoilt little brat you've always been. You ran away rather than face up to the responsibility of being my wife. You still don't want to face up to that responsibility.'

Behind her the placid river slid by and overhead somewhere a skylark was singing as it ascended. The warm air was heavy with the scent of many flowers, of the earth and of ripening vines, yet they faced each other like sworn enemies across the width of the stone path.

'Responsibility!' Elaine nearly choked on the word. 'My responsibility as your wife—that's all I seem to have heard about since I came back. If you think I'm so bad at being your wife why don't you divorce me?'

For a moment short thick eyelashes hid Yvan's dark blue eyes as he considered her question. Then a faint smile lifted one corner of his mouth as he looked at her again.

'Because I'm damned if I'm going to make it possible for you to marry someone called *Gerald,*' he replied mockingly.

'Oh, you're saying that to put me off! That isn't your reason at all. It's because you want Chambourtin, and the way Uncle Armand's will stands now you're bound to get half of it,' she retorted.

He stared at her narrowly, then shrugged his shoulders as if he considered further argument a waste of time. His glance drifted over her, lingered on the wet drooping rose at her bosom.

'You look a mess and you stink of the river,' he said irrelevantly.

'Oh! Thank you for nothing,' she seethed, and turning away she began to walk along the path, feeling small sharp stones prick the bare soft soles of her feet.

'Where are your shoes?' he barked after her, and she stopped to look back at him.

'I left them in the boat when I decided to swim for it,' she replied, tilting her chin disdainfully, and turning her back on him she continued on her painful way. Yvan soon caught up with her, guiding the bicycle along with one hand on the centre of the handlebars.

'You shouldn't have left the boat—you broke a safety rule by doing that,' he reprimanded her. 'You should have stayed in it. You could have been drowned.'

'I could have also been drowned going over the weir,' she replied.

'The weir?' he repeated. 'Which weir?'

'The one further down the river. I could hear it.'

'In your imagination,' he scoffed. 'The only weir is near the village of Loutin, and that's about seven kilometres from here. Before you'd gone that far the boat would have come to rest somewhere against a bank where the river curves and you would have been able to step ashore and walk back to the chateau with your shoes on.'

Elaine had no doubt that he was right. Having grown up in the district he knew the river and its ways much better than she did. Once again she had behaved impulsively, without thinking, and now she was having to walk along this stony path in bare feet. She glanced sideways. At the edge of the path there was a narrow strip of long grass. It would hurt her feet less if she walked on that, she decided, and stepped on to it.

'If you'd like to sit on the crossbar of the bike I'll

ride you back to the house,' offered Yvan quietly. 'I haven't time to walk back with you.'

She stopped and looked at the bike. It was a handsome streamlined affair, glinting red and silver in the sunlight. It wasn't the same one he had used last year. He had always used a bicycle to get about the vineyards because a bicycle could go where a motorised vehicle couldn't go. It did not pollute the air nor damage the precious vines and it gave him the same exercise that walking did, at the same time allowing him to cover the whole extent of the estate in one day.

'I can manage by myself, thank you,' she replied stiffly. 'Don't let me keep you.' And she set off again, almost crying out as she stepped on a sharp twig hidden in the long grass that stabbed her foot like a knife. Standing on one leg, she raised her foot to examine the damage. A small hole had been made, from which blood was beginning to seep slowly.

'*Mon dieu,*' rasped Yvan, 'how stubborn you are! And you always put yourself first. You never consider anyone else or how you might inconvenience anyone by your foolish impetuous actions.'

'All right,' she cried, suddenly very near to tears because her foot really did smart from the sharp jab and because his sudden harsh criticism of her was finding an echo in her conscience. 'Rub it in! I'm selfish, stubborn and foolish, but I just can't see how I'll cause anyone inconvenience by walking back to the house.'

'You'll get bloody feet,' he replied curtly. 'You'll cut them to pieces. A short distance you might have managed, but not two and a half kilometres, which is about the distance from here on foot.' He paused, then added more softly, 'Come on, Elaine. It won't be the first time we've doubled up on a bicycle.'

It was true. Many times before they had married

and afterwards he had given her a lift when he had come across her walking in some part of the estate, and it was possible that it was memories of those times which were making her awkward now, because sitting on the crossbar would bring them into close physical contact and already once this morning Elaine had discovered what close contact with him could do to her.

She looked along the path where it wound beside the river, dipping and rising as it followed the contours of the land. She thought of the distance to the chateau, saw the small stones sharp and glittering, and imagined how sore her feet would be. She felt the heat of the sun on her uncovered head and her bare arms and imagined how hot and exhausted she would be at the end of her walk; and her opposition to his suggestion collapsed.

'Very well,' she said coolly, and moving across to the bike she perched herself on the crossbar. At once Yvan swung his leg over behind the bike and sat on the seat. His arms came round her as he reached for the handlebars. Elaine felt the warm hairiness of his chest left bare by the opening of his shirt, which he had unbuttoned to the waist for coolness, brush against her bare arm.

Then with one foot still on the ground and the other on a pedal he began to push the bike forwards and she felt his breath warm her neck and the hard thrust of his jaw against her head as he gained balance. He shifted his foot from the ground to the other pedal and they were off.

CHAPTER FOUR

UNDER the fluttering shadows of poplars and aspens, beside the broad shining stretches of the river they rode along the path. Above in the clear air the skylark still sang cheerfully and from out of a cloudless sky the sun blazed down.

The path went up a low hill and Elaine heard Yvan breathing hard as he pedalled. She supposed she should have offered to get off and walk up it, she thought, too late as usual, for they were over the crest and were freewheeling, the warm air whipping past their faces.

Once again she was a lady in some tale of chivalry; the Lady Elaine from Chambourtin. And she had just been rescued from a watery grave in the river by a knight from the Duchess of Aquitaine's court of love. He had taken her up in front of him on his trusty horse and was carrying her back to the chateau where she would reward him by granting him a favour.

Her flight of fancy ended abruptly as Yvan braked suddenly, and she was jerked back against him and the breath was knocked out of her by a collision with his hard sturdy body.

'What happened?' she asked.

'We were going downhill too fast and might have ended in a heap at the bottom,' he replied calmly, beginning to pedal again as the path became level once more.

'Am I too heavy?' she asked.

'*Non*. You're as light as a feather,' he replied, and

began to hum a strangely sad little tune which sounded vaguely familiar.

'What's the song?' she asked.

'It's called *À la Claire Fontaine.* It's very old. It came into my mind when I saw you in the river.'

This was a new aspect of him, one she hadn't met before, and she was suddenly intrigued.

'Please tell me the words,' she asked.

'The first verse only,' he said. 'When you hear them you'll understand why I thought of it.

'À la claire fontaine.
M'en allant promener,
J'ai trouvé l'eau si belle
Que je m'y suis baigné.'

To translate the words into English was to destroy their true poetry, thought Elaine, smiling to herself, but the sense was clear enough. *When I was at the clear spring the water looked so inviting that I went for a swim.*

'You find it appropriate?' asked Yvan.

'Yes, I suppose it is. Are there any more verses?'

'*Oui,* but not about swimming.'

'What are they about then?'

'About past love. There's a refrain which comes after all of them. It goes like this:

'Il y a longtemps que je t'aime, Jamais ne t'oublierai.'

The deep, slightly breathless voice stopped and the words echoed through Elaine's mind as she gazed at the path ahead of them; *It is a long time that I have loved you, Never shall I forget you.*

Trees, river, pathway all blurred before her as her eyes filled with tears. If only Yvan meant those words he had just sung to her! If only he had written them in that letter she had received from him asking her to come back to him she would have returned straight away. If only he loved her—but he didn't and he never had. He loved a woman called Solange, always had and always would.

'It's a pretty song, but it's sad,' she said.

'*Oui,* it's sad. But then to be always sighing and regretting a love affair which is over and done with would make anyone sad. It would also be a waste of time and energy,' he replied with a touch of scorn.

'And you wouldn't do anything like that, would you?' she retorted scathingly.

'*Mais non,* I'm a practical man and believe in taking action,' he said with a chuckle of laughter.

He hadn't taken action when she had left him nine months ago, so he was presumably referring to his affair with Solange. When his past love turned up, instead of wasting time and energy regretting he was married he had taken action, all right. His marriage vows had meant nothing, apparently.

Yet this morning his mother had mentioned that he was unhappy. Why? What would make him unhappy if he wasn't sighing over a past love affair? Elaine frowned suddenly, remembering how Yvan had admitted to having drunk too much the night before he was due to meet her; then how he hadn't overtaken her to stop her on the way. If she hadn't driven into the ditch she might never have been warned about her uncle's change of attitude towards her. She might now have been on her way back to England, thrown out on her ear for having refused to be reconciled with her husband.

Adding all that up, didn't it mean that Yvan didn't want her back at Chambourtin and that was why he was unhappy? He didn't want her back, yet he didn't want a divorce either. Why?

The answer was plain in her mind and gave her no comfort. It was a simple case of wanting his cake and eating it too. While he was married to her he had a chance of inheriting a share in Chambourtin, so he didn't want a divorce, and while she stayed away from him he could visit his mistress without any interference or comment.

The bicycle came to a juddering stop, putting an end for the time being to her unpleasant thoughts. She looked round and saw they had reached the jetty. The path which led up to the house through the vines sloped up steeply to the right, dry and stony.

Yvan swung off the seat of the bicycle and held it steady, one hand on a handlebar and the other at the back of the saddle.

'Sit on the saddle now and I'll push you the rest of the way. The path is too steep for me to ride up with you on as well,' he said crisply.

Elaine slid off the crossbar, her glance going to his face. As usual it betrayed nothing of what he was feeling or thinking. It was hard to imagine that he had just recently sung to her the poignant refrain of a love song. There was only an impression of weary patience that she had noticed in the woods yesterday while he had waited for her to decide what to do, making her feel as if she were a nuisance to him; a nuisance he would like very much to be rid of yet couldn't be, because without her he couldn't, as Solange had put it, better himself.

'Yvan, I know you're busy . . .' she began, pride stepping in.

'So waste no more of my time by arguing with me,' he interrupted curtly. 'Get on the saddle. I have to go up to the house anyway.'

'I could ride up myself,' she protested.

His glance went to her feet, then came up back to her face. He gave an exasperated sigh.

'The pedals on this bike are serrated and would hurt your feet almost as much as walking on the stones of the path would. And the sooner you stop trying to do the opposite to what I want to do the sooner we shall come to some compromise.'

'Compromise?' she echoed. 'Oh, I doubt if we'll ever come to a compromise. You're too inflexible.'

'And you're too damned changeable,' he retorted. 'One of us has to remain consistent. Now get on the saddle. It's almost noon and I have a lot to do before lunch.'

Elaine looked at the pedals, looked at the path. He was right as usual, damn him for his arrogance. She sat on the saddle and held her feet away from the pedals. Yvan reached in front of her to take the other handlebar and began to push. Elaine swayed back precariously as the bike mounted the steep incline, and she had to clutch hold of his denim shirt to keep steady.

And so the Lady Elaine entered the courtyard of the Chateau Chambourtin riding astride her knight's trusty horse while he led it in. And all the other ladies and knights came out to cheer her return.

Again her flight of fancy came to an abrupt end, because instead of people cheering there were only the geese poking curiously about a red Renault that was parked beside the lily pond.

'Oh, I'd forgotten about the Renault,' exclaimed Elaine as the bike stopped. She let go of Yvan's shoulder and slid to the ground.

'I thought perhaps you had,' he commented dryly. 'What are you going to do about it?' he asked, wheeling the bike away to lean it against the wall of the house. He took a large red and white handkerchief from his trouser pocket and began to mop the sweat from his face and neck.

'Do? What do you mean?' she asked.

'You either continue to hire it ... which will cost you money. Or you return it to the agency you hired it from,' he replied with a touch of impatience, then added jeeringly, 'Another responsibility, Elaine. Something about which you'll have to make a decision.'

'Is there a branch of that agency near here?' she asked tentatively.

'How should I know? I don't hire cars. Didn't you ask at the airport where you hired it?'

'No, I didn't think...!'

'You never do,' he mocked.

'Oh, stop needling me,' she countered. 'I expected to return to England on Monday and that I'd drive up to Paris tomorrow afternoon.'

'And aren't you?'

'Of course I'm not. I said I'd stay as long as is necessary, until my uncle dies,' she said, and her voice faded to a whisper as she said the last words.

'And after that?' he insisted.

Of course he would have a vested interest in knowing whether she was going to stay longer.

'I don't know. It all depends. Oh, please try to understand that I can't make a reasonable decision about staying here on a permanent basis yet. There's so much to consider.'

'Judging by what I know about you you're incapable of making any sort of reasonable decision,' he retorted cynically. 'All you ever do is react or over-react emotionally to any given situation whether you've imagined it or whether it's real. You did that nine months ago. You did it just now when you jumped from the boat.' He made an irritated impatient gesture with one hand. 'But this isn't the place to discuss the matter. You need a bath and a change of clothes after being in the river, and I want to go and see Paul Sevigny.'

As he turned away she followed him, obeying a sudden urge to appease him, to show him that she wasn't always thoughtless.

'Yvan, I'm sorry I've been a nuisance this morning. Thank you for letting me ride with you.'

He half-turned to her, but before he could say anything Marguerite came through the tower door.

'Ah, Elaine, what have you been doing now? Why are you in such a mess?' she exclaimed, throwing up her hands.

'I've been in the river,' said Elaine, aware that Yvan had swung on to the bike again and was cycling out of the courtyard. She went on to explain how she had come to be in the river.

'What a nuisance you are,' scolded Marguerite severely. 'You're always in mischief, like a child. It's time you grew up, *ma mie*. *Faugh,* you smell like a swamp! Go upstairs at once and take off those smelly clothes and bring them down to the wash room. Marie has just started the washing. *Vite,* hurry up! Armand is awake and is asking to see you.'

Feeling very much like a child who has caused a great deal of unnecessary trouble, Elaine ran up the stairs to her room, stripped the damp smelly clothes off, slipped into her housecoat and ran downstairs again to the wash room where Marie was helping a middle-aged washerwoman to sort whites from coloureds.

Back upstairs she bathed quickly, washed her hair, dressed in a cotton wrap-round skirt and matching blouse, rubbed her hair as dry as she could and went along to her great-uncle's room.

He didn't look any different from the way he had looked the day before, but his eyes showed recognition when she spoke to him and he reached out a hand to her.

'So you've come back at last, *ma mie,*' he croaked. 'You were a naughty girl to run away. But now you're going to stay, eh?'

Bewildered, Elaine glanced at Marguerite for guidance.

'He has forgotten you came yesterday,' whispered Marguerite. 'You mustn't mind. His memory isn't as it used to be. He'll say the same things over and over to you. You'll have to be patient. It won't be for long.'

'Yes, I'm going to stay, Uncle,' Elaine replied clearly, squeezing his hand. 'I'm going to stay with you.'

'And with Yvan, with your husband? A wife should be with her husband. I've no time for these modern marriages, one day on, next day off. I've no time for some modern wives either. Do you hear me, Elaine? Running off as soon as they discover marriage isn't all kisses and sex. Now let me hear you say you're going to stay with him and never run away from him again.'

His voice was much stronger today, she thought, and he sounded much more like the great-uncle she knew.

'Yes, I'm going to stay with Yvan,' she said, aware that Marguerite was watching and listening.

'*Eh bien,* now I can rest in peace,' murmured Armand, closing his eyes. 'I've been very worried about you, *ma fille*. I was beginning to think I'd have to change my will again.' He opened his eyes and focused them on her. 'I can see your hair shining in the sunlight. You're a pretty child, but wilful like your grandmother was. She wanted you to have Chambourtin. I kept telling her it was too much for a little girl like you, but she never understood how hard it was for me to keep it going.' He closed his eyes again. 'You haven't got the strength or the knowledge,' he murmured. 'You need someone like Yvan, someone who knows about the vines. He's a good man, you know. That's why I arranged it.'

'Arranged what, Uncle?' she asked, completely bewildered by his rambling talk.

'Your marriage. I did it for the best. It was the only way. I wasn't able to marry Marguerite until it was too late for us to have children, so this was the only way, the only way . . .' His voice faded and his hand grew lax as his little spurt of energy left him.

Elaine glanced across at Marguerite who was now sitting by a window sewing her quilt and no longer seemed interested in what was going on at the bedside. Gradually Elaine withdrew her hand from Armand's, and rising to her feet stepped quietly across to Marguerite's side.

For a moment she stood looking out at the river shining blue and silver between its green banks. It seemed it was true that her marriage had been arranged, but would Armand have arranged it without the encouragement of the cool managing woman who sat placidly sewing?

'Uncle Armand is asleep again,' she said.

'It's best that he should be. Soon he'll sleep to wake no more,' Marguerite sighed. 'Ah, *mon pauvre* Armand,' she whispered. 'He has had so much illness in his life and so little true happiness.'

Elaine looked sideways and studied for a while the fine features. Questions were buzzing in her mind which had to be asked and answered some time. Perhaps now?

'This morning Yvan told me that his father was drowned in the river,' she said. 'How did it happen?'

Marguerite's upward glance was surprised. She looked down at her sewing again and snipped off a cotton thread she had been using before answering.

'Do you remember Jean?' she asked.

'Not very well. He did not come to the chateau much, did he?'

'No, and when he did it was usually to talk to Armand. But you must have seen him walking about the vineyards.'

Elaine pondered. 'Maybe I did, was he a bit like Yvan?'

'*Oui*. The same build, the same broad shoulders and deep chest and sturdy legs, but different in the face.'

'Then perhaps I do remember him, just. But he never spoke to me.'

'No, that would be his way. He didn't like your grandmother and he saw you as belonging to her.'

'Oh. Why didn't he like her?'

'She was once very rude to me in his hearing and he never forgave her,' said Marguerite, smiling a secret reminiscing smile. 'He was fiercely independent and a republican to his backbone. He didn't like Eleanor because she considered the St Vérains to be superior to every other vineyard owner here, just because they'd been at Chambourtin for hundreds of years.'

'Yet he didn't object to working for Uncle Armand,' Elaine pointed out.

'Ah, but that was another matter entirely,' said Marguerite. 'His drowning was an accident. Every spring the river floods, but some springs it's worse than others. Fifteen years ago the river was so swollen it flooded the village. Jean went to help rescue people from their homes. A child fell from a window into the torrent which swept down the main street, and its mother screeched to Jean to save the child. He tried and while he was leaning from his punt to grab the child he fell overboard and was swept away too.'

'How dreadful!' Elaine's exclamation rang out sincerely. 'You must have been very upset.'

'Yes, I was. Jean was a fine man. We'd been very happy together,' replied Marguerite, and having threaded her needle with more thread began to sew again.

'I was told once ... that you married him for convenience,' said Elaine in a rush, before she could change her mind.

'But of course I did,' replied Marguerite equably. 'I wanted to live with him, and in my day it was more convenient to be married to a man if you wanted to do that.' She shrugged her slim shoulders. 'Today, it is different.'

'Did you love him?'

'Love? *Hé, hé,* what is love? A matter of opinion? A strong magnetic attraction of two opposites? A willingness to forgive and forget faults, to accept change? You have your definition, I have mine. According to mine I loved Jean. We had a good life together and reared a fine family, two daughters and a son.'

Elaine looked away out of the window again, trying to work up the courage to ask her next question. She had met Yvan's sisters—they had come to the wedding. They were older than he was and both married. One lived in Poitiers and the other at La Rochelle.

'Tante Marguerite, forgive me for asking, but I must know. According to your definition do you also love my great-uncle?'

'But of course. Would I sit with him every day if I didn't?'

'No, I suppose you wouldn't.' Elaine bit her lip. She wasn't really finding out what she wanted to find out. 'Did you love him before you met Jean?' she added quickly.

Marguerite's fine dark eyes came up to meet hers. There was no smile in them.

'Bring a chair and sit down, *petite*. I think it's time I spoke to you frankly and cleared up a few misconceptions that you have and which were, perhaps, put in your mind by your grandmother,' she said.

'Oh, no, it wasn't her. She didn't tell me anything about you,' replied Elaine hastily, defending her beloved grandmother as she brought a chair over to the window. 'It was someone else; someone I met after I married Yvan.' She sat down in the chair and leaned forward with her elbows on her knees and her face resting on her hands. 'I really know nothing about any of you. You see, I was too young to notice much when I used to come with Grand'mère—much about people, I mean. And last summer...' she broke off. All last summer and last autumn she had been living under the spell of romance and had been blind and deaf.

'Then it looks as if I'll have to begin at the beginning, doesn't it?' said Marguerite gently. 'When I was a young woman I trained to be a nurse. For a while I worked in a hospital at Poitiers, and it was there that I met Armand. He was a patient in a surgical ward where I was working. We became friendly and when he was discharged after his operation he invited me to visit him at Chambourtin. I had heard of the place and was naturally very flattered to be invited to go and stay at the chateau, although my parents weren't very pleased because Armand was much older than I and was a bachelor living alone. Also I had been brought up in the Protestant faith, my family having always been Huguenots, whereas the St Vérains had always been Catholics.'

Marguerite's needle flew in and out of the fine material several times, and Elaine watched and waited.

'Once when I came to the chateau Eleanor was here with her English husband and her little boy, your father. I sensed at once that she didn't approve of Armand's friendship with me, and she soon made it clear that I wasn't welcome here because I wasn't good enough to be a friend of her dear brother. I was a little hurt, and when Armand invited me again I decided not to come. Then one day when I was leaving the hospital I was surprised to find him waiting for me in his car. He asked me to go for a drive with him—I did, and he asked me to marry him. I declined.'

'Oh, why?'

'I'd met someone else whom I liked better, a man who was very different from Armand, stronger, more spirited.'

'Jean Durocher?'

'*Oui.* He was the younger of two sons. His father owned a vineyard near Bellic, nothing like the size of Chambourtin but a good acreage which produces fine grapes. The Durochers were known to be hardworking and very knowledgeable about viticulture. In due course Jean asked me to marry him and I accepted. We were married in my home town, forty years ago this month.'

'What did Uncle Armand do?' asked Elaine, who was by now fascinated by Marguerite's love story.

'He sent us a lovely wedding gift and said nothing, at least not for a while. He was having problems, you see, here with the vineyard. Because he wasn't very strong he wasn't able to supervise the cultivation himself, and gradually the quality of the grapes Chambourtin produced declined, with the result that the quality of the brandy declined also. It looked very much as if the St Vérain brandy was going to lose its position as one of the best in the world, and there was danger of its being excluded from the hierarchy of the brandy industry. It was then that Armand approached Jean and asked him to take over the management of the Chambourtin vineyard.'

'Were you pleased?'

'For Jean, yes. It meant recognition of his abilities and it also meant that we would be better off. For although he and his brother Pierre had equal shares in the Durocher vineyard it wasn't really big enough to support both of them. Armand's offer was a challenge to him. He retained his share in the Durocher property but he came here to work. We moved into a cottage on the estate and our children were born here. Many years later Armand asked me to take over the position of housekeeper of the chateau, and much later, three years after Jean's death, Armand asked me to marry him. After some hesitation I agreed. You see, *ma chère,* all those years after I had refused him he had never bothered with any other woman, and I felt I owed it to him to give him a little happiness . . .'

'I understand,' said Elaine. Her romantic heart was touched by the story of her great-uncle's faithfulness in love even after the woman he had loved had married someone else. 'Thank you for telling me. The person who told me the story had it all wrong—she told me you'd married Jean so you could live near Armand. But if Jean didn't work at Chambourtin when you married him that couldn't have been so, could it?'

Marguerite's eyes narrowed and her mouth curved

in a sardonic expression which gave her a fleeting resemblance to Yvan.

'No, it wasn't so. In fact it was the other way round. One of the reasons why Armand wanted Jean to take over the management of the vineyards here was so that I would come to live at Chambourtin and he would at least see me occasionally, although I didn't know that until he told me years afterwards. Whoever told you differently was telling a deliberate lie, possibly to discredit me and make me seem a little less in your eyes.'

Elaine had too little experience in disguising her reactions to pretend that the shrewd observation wasn't correct. Colour stormed into her pale cheeks and her glance wavered. She looked down at her hands and nodded.

'It would be interesting to know why she did it.' Marguerite laughed suddenly. 'You see, I've guessed it was a she. Only a woman would say something damaging about another woman. It would be her way of getting her revenge. It's the action of a woman who has been scorned in some way, who has been rejected.' Marguerite laughed again as Elaine gave her an alarmed upward glance. 'Don't look so worried,' she said. 'I'm not a fortune-teller or a witch. I just have much experience of people and how they behave. It was Solange Bourget who discussed me with you, wasn't it?'

Again Elaine could only nod dumbly, and this time Marguerite didn't laugh but sighed rather wearily.

'I was afraid of that. I should have warned you about her at the time. Her sudden befriending of you worried me. But you seemed so happy with Yvan and I thought love would protect you.' Marguerite lifted her shoulders in a shrug as if she could no longer be bothered. Fatigue had made her face very pale and drawn. Looking at her, Elaine felt a twinge of conscience followed by a great desire to do something to make amends for having been so prejudiced against her mother-in-law.

'You're very tired,' she said. 'If you would like to go and rest I'll sit with my uncle for a while. Just tell me what to do if he should wake and need anything.'

'That's kind of you, Elaine. Ah, it was a bad night. I'll do as you suggest if you'll promise to wake me if something unusual occurs.'

'Yes, I promise,' said Elaine.

'If he wakes up just sit beside him. Listen to him, hold his hand, show you care. If he seems in pain let me know or wake the other nurse—she's sleeping in the next room. I'll tell Jacques to bring your lunch to you. I expect you, who are so full of life, will find sitting here hour after hour a little tedious.'

'I expect I shall,' agreed Elaine with a smile, 'but I think it's time I learned to do something for others.'

Marguerite smiled at her and leaned forward to kiss her on the cheek.

'You are here and we are glad that you are, all of us, *chérie*. And I hope that you meant what you said just now when you said you're going to stay. You belong here,' she said softly.

She went from the room, and after taking her chair back to the bedside Elaine selected a magazine from the pile in the bedside cupboard. She had flipped through several glossy pages before she realised she wasn't concentrating on the contents of the magazine and put it back on the pile.

Her mind was too full of conflicting thoughts for her to read. For instance, if she had known the truth about Marguerite's marriage to Jean Durocher she would have known that Solange had not been telling the truth. Did it follow then that if she had caught Solange telling one lie she would have been suspicious of anything else she had said?

Once again her mind flicked back to that scene in Solange's apartment. She had doubted what Solange had said, she remembered; she had said, frantically almost, 'I don't believe you,' several times. It had been when she had seen the solid evidence of Yvan's gloves and lighter that her trust in him had wavered.

Now she closed her eyes briefly as once again she was riven by the raw pain she had experienced at the time. Marguerite had just said that she had hoped love would have protected her, but it hadn't. She had been terribly hurt because the one person in the world to whom she had given herself wholeheartedly had betrayed her trust in him so soon after their marriage. Instead of protecting her, love had turned to rage. She had wanted to hurt Yvan. That was why she had run away without a word of explanation. But she had hoped deep down that he would follow her, explain away the evidence of the gloves and lighter, swear that he loved only her and that Solange meant nothing to him, and plead with her to return. He hadn't followed her and nothing had been explained.

The door opened and Jacques appeared with a tray which he set down on a small table that he drew up beside her. Elaine talked to him for a few minutes about the condition of her uncle. When Jacques had gone she ate the beautifully cooked meal sent up by Berthe the cook. There was a bowl of delicious Vichyssoise soup, a chicken salad, a *compôte de fruit* and a small pot of coffee.

She had just finished eating when the door opened and Yvan entered the room, bringing with him the scents of the vineyard and the smell of tobacco smoke.

He stood by the bed, a strong virile presence in faded blue, his health and vigour seeming to mock the fragile figure on the bed.

'He's sleeping very peacefully as if all his troubles are over at last,' he said. 'Maybe he thinks they are now that you've come back and you've said you're staying.' He glanced across at her.

'You don't want me to stay, do you?' she challenged quietly, staring steadily at him. 'You didn't want me to come back at all.'

'What makes you think that?' he queried.

'You didn't want to meet me off the plane.'

'Now what's got into you?' he demanded roughly. 'I've told you why I was late ...'

'But you didn't tell me why you drank too much the night before.'

'*Mon dieu,* does there have to be a reason? I was with an old friend. We did our two years' army service together. I hadn't seen him for a long time. I took him a bottle of cognac as a present, and we drank the lot for no other reason than we were glad to see each other.'

'But yesterday when I asked you why you didn't overtake me and stop me, you told me that the reason for that could be the same reason for your drinking too much the night before,' she began.

'No, I didn't say that. I said the answer to both questions could be the same, such as *I don't know why*!' His mouth curved in a derisive grin. 'You're doing it again, *chérie*. Imagining and then reacting to what you've imagined.'

'I'm not,' she argued crossly, 'I'm trying to get at the truth. You don't want me here, yet you won't agree to a divorce and I'd like to know why, but you keep dodging round the issue.'

These are just six special occasions in a romantic lifetime – but perhaps the most important six . . .

1. First date
2. Engagement
3. Wedding breakfast
4. First Wedding Anniversary
5. First Baby
6. Silver Wedding Anniversary

RULES

1. The instructions on the previous page form part of the rules.
2. The Competition is open to any Mills & Boon reader who is resident in the United Kingdom or Eire, except employees (and their families) of Mills & Boon and any other person directly concerned with the competition.
3. All entries must be on an official entry form and be written in ink or ball point pen in block capitals. Any which are not clearly legible or with omissions or otherwise not conforming to the rules of the competition will not be considered.
4. Each entry must be accompanied by three Mills & Boon rose tokens. (Except for the fourth entry which requires only one additional token.)
5. No responsibility will be accepted for any entries lost, delayed, mislaid or damaged in the post. Proof of posting will not be accepted as proof of receipt.
6. All entries must be received by the last post on 30th November 1977.
7. The Judges will examine all entries. The first prizes will be awarded to the entrants who in the opinion of the Judges have most suitably matched the special occasions and the meals, and who have completed the sentence 'Mills & Boon and Romantic Meals' in the most romantic and original way. Second prizes will be awarded to the next ten most meritorious entries.
8. The judges decision will be final and legally binding. No correspondence will be entered into. No competitor may win more than one prize.
9. Prizewinners will be notified by post and announced in the Competitors Journal.
10. Entries become the property of Mills & Boon and will not be returned under any circumstances.
11. All entries must be sent pre-paid post to the competition address. Entrants wishing to obtain a full list of prizewinners should include a large stamped addressed envelope with their entries marked 'Winners'.

	1st	2nd	3rd	4th
a) A Coffee Bar				
b) A Disco				
c) A Local Hotel				
d) A Pub Snack				
e) An Exclusive Restaurant				
f) A Family Dinner Party				
No. of tokens required	3	6	9	10

Name ______________________

Address ______________________

____

____

Now complete the following sentence in the most romantic and original way:
'Mills & Boon and Romantic Meals

____

____

____

(in not more than 10 words).

Post your entry to: Mills & Boon,
Romantic Meals Competition,
PO Box 6, Kettering, Northants.

Closing date: 30th November 1977

Offer open to UK residents only

'Quietly!' he admonished her, a finger to his lips. 'You'll disturb your uncle. This isn't the place for us to be discussing our marital difficulties.'

'Oh, you!' she seethed, and springing to her feet she walked over to the window to stand staring out blindly.

Yvan followed her and as soon as he leaned against the window frame she was aware of him, intensely, quiveringly aware of his warmth and vitality; but she kept her face averted. Her chin was held high, her small nose tilted in the air, her soft mouth compressed and her long eyelashes drooping disdainfully.

Yvan said something and at once she abandoned her pose of disdain, turning to look curiously at him. Arms folded across his chest, he was looking at her with eyes which gleamed derisively between narrowed lids.

'La Belle Dame sans merci,' he drawled. 'I was making a comment on how you looked just now with your nose in the air, as if you were *la grande dame* looking down on the earthy peasant. Have you decided what you're going to do about the Renault yet?'

She hadn't, of course. She had forgotten all about it again. Disconcerted by his comment about how she had looked, she glanced away from him out of the window.

'Should I have decided?' she countered weakly.

'Which means you haven't, I suppose,' he mocked. 'Then maybe I can help you to decide. There is a branch of the agency at a garage in Angoulême. I've just phoned them and was told that if you'd like to take the car to them this afternoon they have someone who can drive it back to Paris airport tomorrow.'

'You're very determined that I should be rid of it,' she challenged.

'I'm a mean and thrifty peasant,' he replied with a

touch of self-mockery, 'I'm only trying to save your money for you. You don't need the car while you stay here. There are other cars you can use if you want to drive anywhere—even if you want to run away again, as you well know, so you can stop thinking that I'm trying to prevent you from leaving when you like by getting rid of the car.'

She flicked a wary sidelong glance at his dark sardonic face. He had just read her mind very accurately.

'I can't go to Angoulême this afternoon. I've promised Tante Marguerite that I'd stay with my uncle so that she can rest,' she muttered.

'Then of course you must stay. I'll take the Renault in for you. I was thinking of going to Angoulême later this afternoon.'

'But how will you get back here if you have to leave the car there?' she exclaimed, and his eyebrows tilted satirically.

'So sometimes you do think ahead,' he mocked. 'Never fear, I shall find a way of coming back.' He paused and his eyes narrowed thoughtfully. 'That is of course if I want to come back tonight. If I decide to stay in Angoulême you can be sure I'll return some time tomorrow, not early because it will be Sunday. Is it settled, then? Shall I take the Renault in for you?'

'Yes, I suppose so,' she replied rather vaguely, because she was suddenly concerned not with the car but with the possibility of him staying the night in Angoulême. To her way of thinking there was only one place where he would stay, and that was at Solange's apartment.

'Then where are the keys?' he asked.

'Still in the car, I expect, unless Marcel gave them to Jacques when he brought it here this morning.'

'I'll go and see,' he said, moving away from the

window. 'I hope you have a good afternoon with your patient. It's kind of you to sit with him while my mother rests. I'll see you later.'

The casual final remark gave her hope.

'Later? Then you'll come back tonight?' she asked as she followed him across the room to the door.

He opened the door and went through then turned to look back at her, his hand on the outside knob. There was a challenging glint in his eyes as they met hers.

'What does it matter to you whether I come back tonight or not?' he said softly. 'You've made it very clear that you prefer to sleep alone. *Au revoir, ma chère femme.*'

The door closed quietly after him. In two strides Elaine reached it, her hand stretched out to grasp the brass knob, ready to turn it and fling the door back so she could go after Yvan.

The cool hard feel of the knob against her palm had a cautionary effect, and instead of turning the knob she stood staring at the white-painted panels of the double doors.

What would she say if she did go after him? Admit that it did matter to her whether he came back tonight or not? Admit that she didn't really want to sleep alone and was willing to share the double bed with him—would do anything, in fact, rather than have him stay the night in Angoulême with Solange?

Her hand left the knob and she turned back into the room. Slowly she paced back to the chair beside the bed and sat down, her eyes wide and unseeing as she faced the truth about herself. Her reaction to his taunting challenge had been instinctive, as usual, but suddenly she knew why she had reacted in that way. She was jealous, and only a woman who was in love with a man and wanted him to be in love with her and no one else would be jealous.

Had nothing changed, then? Had all her attempts during the past nine months to forget Yvan been ineffectual? She had thought she had succeeded. She had thought she had fallen out of love with him and was on the verge of falling in love with another man. Yet she hadn't been back in Chambourtin twenty-four hours and Yvan was filling her whole mind, pushing everyone and everything else out of it just as he had twelve months ago when she had returned to Chambourtin after an absence of nearly nine years and had met him for the first time. Big, sensual, enigmatic, he had stepped into her life then and had possessed her in every way. Now it looked as if he was going to take over again, in spite of all her efforts to resist his domination.

'Elaine? Are you still there?'

Armand's voice was a thin thread of sound in the room where only the ticking of the antique ormolu clock on the marble mantelpiece above the wide fireplace broke the warm silence of the afternoon.

'Yes, Uncle.' She leaned forward and took his hand in hers.

'Good, I'm glad you've stayed. I have much to tell you. It's about my will,' he muttered.

'It doesn't matter, Uncle. You don't have to tell me anything. You mustn't distress yourself by talking about it,' she said.

'*Mais oui,* it is very necessary that I do,' he retorted rather breathlessly. 'That is why I asked Marguerite to send for you. I want you to stay here with Yvan. I want you to stay married to him. If you run away from him again or if you divorce him, my plan will have failed and Chambourtin will pass into the hands of strangers.

Elaine, it all depends on you. I want you to stay and carry on the traditions of our family. But you can't do it without Yvan's help.' He paused and tried to clear his throat, wheezing for breath.

'Please don't talk any more, Uncle,' Elaine urged anxiously. 'Let me talk instead and tell you about my work. You'll be pleased with me. I'm becoming very knowledgeable about wine. Charles says he thinks I'm quite a good wine taster.'

He nodded, smiling a little.

'I'm pleased to hear it. That's the St Vérain blood showing. But you must have a child, Elaine—no, several children—you and Yvan. If you'd stayed you'd have been expecting by now and I'd have seen my dream come true. I'll never understand why you ran away from Yvan. I don't understand the ways of young women today, but you've come back now and if he's the man I believe him to be he won't let you go again. Stay with him and Chambourtin might have an heir.' He sighed sadly and his hand tensed weakly on hers. 'I'd have liked to have held yours and Yvan's child in my arms, *chérie*, but I know I won't be here when it's born.'

Elaine swallowed and sniffed. She had a feeling she was going to cry.

'I'd like to have a child some day,' she murmured, knowing he was expecting her to answer him and yet reluctant to commit herself to a promise. 'But it isn't always possible.'

He jerked his head up from the pillow and peered at her.

'What do you mean, it isn't possible? You're a healthy young woman, aren't you? And Yvan is virile with strong sexual appetites. You're not going to tell me that you're frigid and that you don't enjoy being made love to, because I won't believe you if you do. Last summer I was always coming across the pair of you somewhere, kissing and fondling, even before you were married.' He paused and his head fell back. 'There is nothing wrong with you, is there, *chérie*? Ah, *mon dieu*, that would be the last straw, for you to be infertile!'

Elaine was glad there was no one else in the room to hear what he was saying or to see how her cheeks had flamed scarlet. No one, least of all someone of the opposite sex, had ever spoken so frankly to her about sex and she could not help feeling surprised that it was her great-uncle, whom she had always regarded as being something of a prude, who was speaking in this way.

'No . . . I don't think I am,' she murmured.

'But you are not sure. Then we shall have Dr Sevrin examine you. There are tests, I understand, that can be done these days to find out if anything is lacking, pills you could take . . .'

'No, oh no, that won't be necessary,' she exclaimed, horrified by what he was suggesting. 'There's nothing wrong with me, honestly, Uncle.'

'Then why did you say it isn't possible for you and Yvan to have a child?' he inquired querulously. 'You're here with him. You're married to him. You're reconciled to him. What is there to stop you from going to bed with him and . . .' He broke off as a spasm of coughing shook him.

Alarmed by the paroxysm, which seemed to be a severe one, Elaine jumped to her feet and leaned over him.

'Please, Uncle, you mustn't get excited. It will be all right, I promise you. Yvan and I will have a child.'

The coughing stopped and he lay there, his thin

wizened chest heaving as he gasped for breath. His face was a strange bluish colour and his lips were bloodless.

'Are you all right? Are you in pain?' whispered Elaine. 'Shall I wake the nurse?'

'No, no.' Armand's hand clung to hers with surprising strength. 'It's past ... I'll be all right ... now you've given me your word. You see, if you and Yvan don't stay together, if you don't have a child my dream won't come true ...' Weak tears began to glisten in his eyes and slide out of their corners on to his cheeks.

'What dream?' she asked.

'The one I've always had, that a child might be born who would have the blood of the St Vérains, my blood, and that of the woman I loved in its veins. She married someone else, you know. She married Jean and I had to worship her from afar like a knight in a tale of chivalry. Do you remember, *ma fille*, the stories I used to tell you about the songs sung by the troubadours in the Age of Romance? They always sang of the love of a knight for the lady who was married to his overlord?'

'Yes, Uncle, I remember,' she said, relieved that his mind had wandered on to a less worrisome subject. 'My favourite was *The Romance of the Rose*.'

'I liked that one too,' he whispered. 'I'd like to sleep now, I'm very tired. I feel I can rest now that I know you and Yvan are going to have a child.'

He dozed off again holding her hand and time ticked by in the warm sunlit room. Elaine sat quietly, her thoughts in a turmoil as the result of the recent conversation which had revealed her uncle as a romantic in the truest sense of the word; loving Marguerite and accepting her marriage to Jean Durocher as inviolable, and yet planning the union of his blood and hers in a fantastic way by arranging a marriage between herself and Yvan.

The clock struck four and the door of the room opened. Marguerite came in and held the door while Marie entered carrying the tea tray.

'Set it on the table by the window, Marie,' instructed Marguerite crisply, and came over to the bedside to look at Armand. Frowning a little, she took his hand from Elaine's loose clasp and felt for his pulse.

'It's very weak,' she exclaimed. 'What has he been doing? Talking?'

'Yes. He talked a lot and he became very excited about his will. I tried to stop him,' explained Elaine anxiously. 'He'll be all right, won't he? I did my best, Tante Marguerite.'

'I hope you didn't argue with him about the will. He gets very confused about it,' said Marguerite, looking at her sternly.

'No, I didn't, but he kept wanting to know why Yvan and I haven't a child. He was most insistent that we should have children. He said his dream wouldn't come true if we didn't.'

'*Hé, hé,*' sighed Marguerite, her expression softening a little as she released Armand's hand. 'He's always talking about that. He seems to think he can organise your lives. Poor Armand—he's such a romantic at heart. But come, *chérie,* and have some tea. I can see it's been difficult for you sitting with him. The talk about a child has upset you.'

Elaine carried her chair across to the window again and watched Marguerite pour the tea.

'Do you have any idea what's in his will?' she asked.

'No. He likes to make a secret of it, although he's always talking about it. He made it last year soon after you and Yvan married. For years he's been saying he would have to make some provision for you so that you could carry on the St Vérain traditions. I know

Eleanor used to worry him constantly about that. She never seemed to understand that times had changed. Did she ever tell you what she wanted for you?'

'She mentioned it once only, and I didn't know what she meant—I was too young at the time to understand. Until last December I never gave it a thought,' replied Elaine. 'Does Yvan know what's in Uncle's will?'

Marguerite picked up her quilting again and the needle flashed in and out of the material. She did not look up and her hand did not falter.

'Possibly, but he's never mentioned it to me. Why don't you ask him yourself if you are troubled about it?' she inquired smoothly. 'Now you've done your good deed for the day, so you can go off and enjoy the rest of the evening.'

Elaine glanced at her watch. Four-thirty. Maybe Yvan hadn't left yet for Angoulême.

'Yes, I think I will,' she said. 'Shall I see you later at dinner?'

'No, tonight I'll eat up here. You and Yvan can dine *tête-à-tête*, or perhaps he'll take you out to dine. You two have much lost time to make up.'

Elaine left the room quickly. She ran along the landing to the stairs and leapt down them two at a time. Unless she was in time to prevent Yvan from leaving for Angoulême there would be no *tête-à-tête* dinner with him for her tonight, no chance to talk and ask all the questions which must be asked.

The need to talk to him was a sudden desperate urge which sent her sprinting across the hall, through the door into the courtyard now full of purple shadow and the heavy scent of flowers.

She was too late. The Renault had gone. For a moment she thought of asking for the loan of her uncle's car and following Yvan to Angoulême to confront him at Solange's apartment.

'Are you looking for Monsieur Yvan?' Jacques had come to the doorway of the tower and was looking out at her.

'Oui.'

'He left about half an hour ago. He won't be back to dinner. Berthe and I are going into the city too. There is a film on at a cinema which we'd like to see and since there will be only yourself dining downstairs tonight we were wondering if you'd mind if we served it a little earlier than usual so that we can be in time for the start of the first showing.'

'Yes, of course. Please serve it as soon as you like. I ... I'm just going to walk in the garden. Call me when you're ready.'

'*Oui, madame*. Thank you.'

CHAPTER FIVE

An hour later, feeling very small and very lonely, Elaine sat at the long dining table in the high-ceilinged, elegantly furnished dining room by herself. It was still light and through the long windows that opened on to the terrace the golden glow of the westering sun shafted in to glint on silver and highly-polished wood.

As always the food was delicious and had been perfectly cooked by Berthe, and Jacques waited on the table with his usual faultless decorum as if Armand or Marguerite were there.

It was all such a lot of trouble to go to for one person, Elaine thought, especially a person like herself who was accustomed to less formality when eating. She could have easily have prepared a meal for herself in the kitchen and eaten it there and then Berthe and Jacques could have gone into Angoulême earlier.

But then it was their job to prepare meals and serve them in this house, and if they didn't do that what would they do? It was just that the formality and Jacques' deference increased her feeling of loneliness, made her feel even more of a nuisance and added to the new feeling which had begun to develop ever since her uncle had told her about his dream, a feeling of being trapppd.

Trapped by the fantastic dream of an old man; trapped in a marriage to a man who didn't love her, so that Uncle Armand could realise his dream of a child being born who would have in its veins his own blood and that of the woman he had always loved.

Elaine lifted the glass of white wine that Jacques had poured for her. It was the third glassful, she realised, one more than she usually allowed for herself, but she hadn't refused when he had offered because she felt a need for something to drug her mind, to make her forget that she was in a trap.

Did Yvan feel trapped too? she wondered hazily. Was that why he drank too much sometimes, because he was trapped in a marriage with a woman he didn't love; trapped by his own ambition? Poor Yvan. Poor Elaine. Both of them trapped. It was enough to make anyone cry.

'I've put the coffee tray in the study, *madame,*' said Jacques at her elbow, and she stared up at him, aware that the wine had gone to her head and that her thoughts had become fussy and sentimental.

'Thank you, Jacques. You and Berthe may go now,' she said, and had to suppress a desire to giggle at the way she had spoken. Very formal, very ladylike. The lady Elaine of Chateau Chambourtin, who dined alone because her husband had gone to visit his mistress.

She felt as if she were floating across the floor to the doorway where Jacques held the door open politely.

'Good night, *madame,*' he said.

She gave him what she was sure was her most dazzling smile.

'Good night, Jacques. I hope you enjoy the film,' she replied, and floated down the corridor to the study which smelt of leather and the smoke of Yvan's after-dinner cigars.

She sat in the chair in which he had sat the previous night and stared at the coffee tray. Last night he had been here, had brought her cognac and had sat with her, in silence it was true, but he had been here. Tonight he was in Angoulême with Solange, while she sat here alone feeling sorry for herself and was just a little tipsy from having drunk too much wine with her dinner.

Leaning forward, she poured coffee into a cup. She didn't add any cream or sugar but drank it black all at once, shuddering at the bitter taste. She set the cup down and the silence of the house seemed to engulf her. Loneliness seemed like a great weight that dragged her down into depression.

She couldn't bear it any more. She had to talk to someone. Now was the time to make her telephone call because there was no one about to overhear what she had to say. She got up from the chair and went over to the desk, noticing that she still felt a little unsteady.

It didn't take long for her to get through to Gerald's flat and she half-sat on the corner of the desk, listening to the ringing tone at the other end of the line and willing him to answer. But no one lifted the receiver and eventually she heard the French operator's voice advising her that there was no answer and to try again later.

Slowly Elaine replaced the receiver. It seemed that Gerald was out too. And why shouldn't he be? After all, it was Saturday night and he could be at a concert or even dining with another woman ... like Yvan.

Deliberately she swerved her thoughts away from the direction they were taking, picked up the receiver again and asked the operator to get her another number in England; her cousin Charles's telephone number. In a few minutes she heard with a sense of relief the receiver being lifted in the house at Ashleigh and the pleasant voice of Jenny, Charles's wife, answering.

'Oh, hello, Elaine,' she said when Elaine had informed her who was calling. 'I was wondering when we'd hear from you. How's your great-uncle?'

'Not very well. I don't think he's going to live much longer.'

'I'm sorry to hear that—he's such a nice old gentleman.'

'Jenny, I won't be coming back just yet.' Elaine spoke quickly. 'I've promised I'll stay until the end. That could be sooner or later, I don't know. You do understand, don't you?'

'Of course I do, love. I'll tell Charles and he can tell them at the office that you won't be back Monday morning.'

'Thank you. I phoned Gerald to tell him, but there was no reply.'

'No, there wouldn't be,' agreed Jenny. 'He's taken a few days off and gone cruising. It was a last-minute decision, I think. Actually he said he might go over to France. Lucy's gone with him.' Lucy was Jenny's youngest daughter, who was a year older than Elaine.

'Oh, I see,' said Elaine blankly.

'I think they've gone because the weather is so glorious. How is it with you?'

'Very dry and hot.'

'Good for the vines, then—which reminds me, how is Yvan?'

'Very well, thank you.'

'Any chance of you and him getting together again?'

'Oh, Jenny, it's impossible to discuss the matter over the phone just now!'

Jenny sounded soothing. 'All right, love, let it go. I was only thinking how nice it would be if you were reconciled. I expect you'll be writing and keeping us informed of your uncle's health. His death will cause quite an upheaval over there, I suppose, since he has no direct heirs.'

'Yes, it will. Goodbye, Jenny.'

'Goodbye, love, and take care.'

Elaine set down the receiver. The conversation had been far from satisfactory and had somehow made her feel lonelier than ever. While she was sitting here alone in this house surrounded by silence and the relics of a way of life that had long since passed away, everyone else was enjoying a Saturday evening out. Berthe and Jacques had gone to the cinema. Marie the maid was probably out, if not with a boy-friend, with her girl-friends. Gerald was sailing off the French coast somewhere, or was possibly ashore in a French port with his friends and Lucy. Yes, she had often noticed how keen Lucy was about Gerald. Perhaps if she hadn't had to come away she would have been invited to go cruising. Perhaps he had only invited Lucy to take her place ... oh, it didn't matter, because what was hurting the most was she was sitting here alone while Yvan was spending his Saturday night in Angoulême with Solange.

Slipping off the desk, Elaine ranged restlessly about the room, wondering how to entertain herself. There was a radio but no television because Uncle Armand didn't like television. She switched on the radio, but could make no sense out of numerous French stations all vying with each other to present records of music, so she switched it off.

If she and Yvan lived here together by themselves it wouldn't be as quiet as this. They would entertain often. They would have children and dogs, the house would vibrate with life.

Elaine clapped her hands to her head which was beginning to ache. It seemed that the wine hadn't done her any good at all, nor had the coffee. She was becoming sentimental again and indulging in wishful thinking. She and Yvan weren't going to have any children, even though she had promised her uncle that they would, because under the present circumstances she couldn't possibly stay at Chambourtin after her uncle Armand's death and live with Yvan as his wife.

She went to the door of the room and flung it open and stepped out into the corridor. There was no help there either, only the silence of a house where illness and probable death lingered. Somewhere a clock chimed the hour: nine. It was early, but she might as well go up to bed as sit in the study struggling to sort out her problems.

She took another bath, more as a form of relaxation and entertainment than anything else; she used plenty of water and stayed a long time in its scented warmth, then after drying herself she dressed in a different nightgown from the one she had worn the previous night. Made from sheer black chiffon nylon, it was full and flowing with long sleeves looped into tight cuffs fastened with tiny pearl buttons. Its neckline was square and the front also fastened with tiny buttons right down below her waistline.

When she was dressed she brushed her hair until it shone like new brass and applied a little scent behind her ears. Then she gazed at her reflection in the long mirror. Her white body gleamed invitingly through the thin material of the nightgown and she thought she looked poised and seductive. She made a face at her reflection. Of what use was it to look seductive when she was going to sleep alone?

Impatiently she switched off the light and went to stand by the open window. Moonlight bleached the dark blue sky and twinkled on the roof of the old *chais*. Calm and warm, full of the scent of roses, it was a perfect summer's night. The only sound was that of a bird singing, a sweet trilling sound, full-throated, coming from the clump of shadowy beech trees, the happy sound of the nightingale.

Enthralled by the sound, Elaine leaned against the window casement, but gradually the birdsong, the scent of many flowers, and the moonlight roused once more her senses of loneliness. It wasn't a night to be spent alone. It was a night to be shared with someone you loved; a night for love.

With a little moan she turned away from the window and crossed to the bed, pulled back quilt and sheets and lay down. For a moment she lay quiet and staring, trying to empty her mind of all thought. Then suddenly she turned her head on the pillow and wept as she had never wept before.

She cried herself to sleep, slipping suddenly into the deep slumber of emotional exhaustion. It was the click of the door closing which roused her. Without moving she lay with her cheek against the damp pillow, wondering whether she had imagined the sound. Then, turning, she almost screamed when she saw a bulky shadow move across the shaft of moonlight that was slanting in through the uncovered window.

'Who's there?' she asked in a tremulous whisper as she sat up.

'C'est moi—Yvan,' replied the shadow in a voice which lilted with surprise.

'What are you doing in here?' she demanded uneasily.

'I could ask you the same,' he retorted with a laugh. He was moving about quietly in the shadows of the room and she realised with a little tingle of alarm that he was undressing.

'You offered to sleep in the other room, remember?' he said. 'I went in there to get my pyjama pants and found the bed empty. You weren't downstairs and you weren't with your uncle, so I thought you must have gone out somewhere. I've come in here to go to bed.' He paused, then added mockingly, 'Does your presence in here mean you've changed your mind yet again and have decided you want to sleep with me after all? Perhaps you want to finish what you started in here this morning.'

Now he was a vague shape against the moonlight which limned the slope of his shoulders and touched to silver his rumpled hair.

'I didn't start anything in here this morning,' she protested.

'Didn't you?' he queried. 'Oh, I had the impression you wanted to make love, but Marie came in with the breakfast tray at that moment. *Eh bien,* if that isn't what you want to do why are you in this bed and not in the other one?'

He had moved again and was now close to the bed beside her. If she reached out she would be able to touch him. The need to touch him, to feel beneath her hands the smooth muscular bulk of him, was an ache somewhere in the region of the pit of her stomach, but she wasn't going to give in to it. She was going to the other room and he could sleep alone.

Quietly she began to slide across to the other side of the bed so that she could leave without running the danger of having to pass close to him. As she felt the mattress sag a little to one side when he sat on it in preparation to lying down, her heart leapt and she moved faster.

'I'd forgotten I'd made that suggestion,' she babbled. 'I'll go now to the other room.'

She slid off the bed and made her way round the end of it to the door, but Yvan had switched on the bedside lamp and when he saw where she was he had also moved quickly and was at the door before her, barring her way, the rosy light from the lamp giving his tanned bare chest the sheen of old copper.

Looking up, Elaine met his heavy-lidded eyes. It seemed to her that a sort of tender mockery twinkled in them. Then she dismissed the idea. It was only the gleam of lamplight reflected in the opaque irises.

'Please let me out,' she said woodenly, looking away from him.

'Not until you've told me why you've been weeping,' he replied softly.

'How do you know I have?'

'The pillow is damp.' He cupped her chin with one hand and forced her face round so he could see it better. 'And your eyelids are swollen. What's wrong, *ma mie*? Were you crying because you were lonely? *Eh maintenant,* you can stop being sad, because I've come back after all...' His arms were around her, drawing her against his bare warmness. She felt his lips against her throat and it seemed to her that the familiar rousing caress had the same quality it had had that morning; as if he knew he had the power to rouse her senses to such a pitch that she would willingly give in to him.

'Oh, stop it!' she cried, pushing at his shoulders with her fists. 'Don't touch me. I can't bear it, knowing you've been with her!'

He raised his head but didn't release her. His hands stayed at her waist. She could feel them hard and possessive through the thin stuff of the nightgown.

'You know with whom I've been?' he asked. 'How do you know? I haven't told you.'

'I didn't need to be told. As soon as you said you were going to Angoulême and might not be back I guessed who you were going to see. You've been with Solange,' she accused breathlessly. 'Oh, how you can dare to come back here, put your arms round me and kiss me when you've been with her I don't know!'

Her breath shuddered with the aftermath of the sobs which had shaken her earlier. Yvan didn't answer her at once but raised a hand to rub at his chin as he considered her with eyes which now looked black.

'I haven't been with Solange,' he replied quietly.

'Then you've been with some other woman ... *aah*!' The cry was wrenched from her as his hand caught her across the cheek. It wasn't a hard slap, just a light flick of his fingers, but for Elaine who was so vulnerable to anything he did or said it was like the flick of a whip. With the back of one hand against her tingling cheek she stared up at him with tears glistening in her eyes. It seemed to her that his face was very stern and hard.

'Why did you do that?' she whispered shakily.

'Because I'm tired of your insults,' he said coldly. His hands left her waist. He leaned back against the door, folded his arms across his chest and surveyed her from under frowning eyebrows. 'Where have you learned to be so insulting?' he rebuked her. 'In England? From your girl friends? Or from this Gerald you were writing to this morning?'

'Insulting?' she repeated in bewilderment.

'*Oui*. In your imagination you're insulting me all the time. Do you think I've no pride, no integrity? I'm not the sort of man who goes with different women all the time. I haven't been with any woman. It's true I called to see Solange because I wanted to ask her a question. There was no answer to my knock and the *concierge* in charge of the apartments told me that

Solange is away, in Paris. I had dinner at a restaurant and then waited for Berthe and Jacques to come out of the cinema so that I could come back with them in my car, which I'd lent to them, just as I'd arranged with them earlier this afternoon.' He drew a deep breath, then expelled it in a weary sigh. '*Eh voilà,* I have done something for you I've never done for any other woman. I've given you an explanation of my movements this evening ... and I've come back. What more can you possibly want, *ma chère femme*?'

'But if Solange had been there you'd have stayed with her,' she accused. 'You stayed with her before. You stayed with her last December when you were supposed to be in Cognac.'

'You know that only because she told you. You took her word for it...' he began, anger beating through his voice.

'No, no, it wasn't just her word,' she said quickly, 'there was evidence. You left your gloves and your cigarette lighter in her apartment. I saw them there.'

His eyes went wide. Still leaning against the door, he stared at her incredulously for a moment, his lower lip caught under the straight edge of his teeth.

'So that was where I left them. I've often wondered,' he said at last, and laughed, a rather dreary sound. He pushed away from the door and stepped past her into the room. Now Elaine could open the door and leave, but suddenly she didn't want to go. Instead she turned to look at Yvan. He was standing by the window looking out. Except for the pyjama shorts he was wearing he was completely bare, and the moonlight silvered his skin, giving him the remote cold appearance of a statue.

'I wish you'd come to me and told me this last year,' he said quietly. 'I could have explained why the gloves and the lighter were in her apartment.'

'Oh, I've no doubt you could have given me some smooth explanation like the one you've given me tonight. And you'd have expected me to accept it without question. Because that's how you believe a wife should behave, isn't it? She should accept your explanations without question even when she knows you're lying.' Elaine's voice shook as she spoke, but at least she had said what had been on her mind all these months. It was out at last instead of going round in her mind like a worm eating at the heart of an apple.

Yvan swung round on her with such savagery in his abrupt movement that she shrank back from him, fearing he might hit her again. He saw her flinch. His eyes narrowed and his mouth twisted.

'No, I'm not going to hit you. I'm not going to give you the chance to add cruelty to your list of insults,' he jeered. He raked long fingers through his hair. 'God, how did we get to such an *impasse*? All I can say is I've never lied to you about why my gloves and lighter were there because you've never given me the chance to lie. You ran away.' He stood for a moment, his chest heaving, his eyes glaring at her, then with a muttered epithet he turned away from her again so that all she could see was the symmetrical shape of his back, narrowing from the wide shoulders to the waist and hips where the band of the shorts had just slipped sufficiently to show a strip of untanned skin.

'Is it permitted that I explain now why my gloves and lighter were in the apartment of Solange?' he asked, swinging round again to look at her.

The polite French phrasing gave his words an irony which was more effective than any angry outburst. It implied that Elaine had been guilty of injustice by not giving him a hearing nine months ago and that by offering to explain now he was conferring an honour on her which she didn't deserve.

'Here and now?' she murmured uneasily, suddenly afraid of what he might tell her.

'*Mais oui,* what better place than in the privacy of our room?'

'It's late and I'm tired,' she evaded.

'Then get into bed. I promise it won't take long.'

'But . . .' she began, and stopped as he moved with that swiftness which always surprised her. He scooped her up into his arms and stepped towards the bed. She had no time to struggle or protest, for within seconds she was dumped unceremoniously on the side of the bed where she had been sleeping and while she was still gasping he took the sheet and the quilt and flung them over her. Then he sat down on the side of the bed close to her.

'Now, are you comfortable and ready to listen?' he asked, his voice hard and cool, the line of his mouth inflexible so that she realised further argument would be useless. He had made up his mind that he was going to explain.

'Yes,' she whispered, pulling the pillow up behind her head, 'I'll listen.'

'*Eh bien,* I'm grateful for a hearing,' he mocked, inclining his head sardonically. 'It is never too late to mend, so I've been told. Like the saying I quoted to you yesterday about the devil—you'd do well to think about it, for I'm about to try and mend our relationship, our marriage, *madame,* which you seem determined to destroy.'

His mockery found its mark and she flinched again. He was putting the blame on her and she supposed he had good reason to. He had good reason also to try and mend their marriage, suggested a malicious little voice inside her, because it was worth his while to stay married to her.

'As you know, last December I spent a few days in Cognac attending a conference,' he said quietly. 'When it was over I drove to Angoulême to visit a small art gallery there where I'd seen some pictures of local scenes on show. I intended to buy one of them as a present for your birthday. While I was there Solange came into the gallery. Naturally I told her why I was there, thinking she might give me some advice. She told me she had just finished a painting of sailing boats in the old harbour of La Rochelle. I remembered how much you'd liked seeing them when we visited the port on our honeymoon, so I went to her studio to see it. I stayed for a while drinking coffee and talking. After all, Solange and I had been good friends once...'

'More than friends, lovers,' Elaine muttered, and his eyes narrowed dangerously. He leaned forward threateningly and placed a hand over her wrist where it lay outside the quilt.

'Are you going to hear me out?' he asked softly, and she nodded quickly and tried to remove her wrist from his grasp, but his fingers tightened around it, so she gave up.

'I don't deny I had an affair with her once, but that was a long time ago when we were younger. It didn't last for long. For me it was a youthful escapade soon forgotten. Solange was always a free spirit, ambitious and independent—she went to Paris to study art, and then we lost touch. I hadn't seen her for almost ten years when she turned up here last autumn.' He shrugged as if to dismiss Solange. 'But to get back to the painting. I liked it and I bought it. If you don't believe me, it's still there in the cupboard, still wrapped up and waiting to be given to you on your next birthday, perhaps, if you're still here. In my haste to leave and come home to Chambourtin I must have left my gloves and lighter behind.'

Moths, attracted by the light, had flown in through the open window and were blundering against the lampshade. Yvan reached out a hand and flicked off the light. Once more the room was silvered and shadowed. Outside the nightingale gave one last sweet trill and was silent.

'Do you believe me?' Yvan said softly, leaning forward so that Elaine felt his breath feathering her cheek. His hand moved caressingly on her wrist against the thin skin over her pulse, sending a tingle of sensual pleasure up her arm.

That tingle was a warning. He was doing it again, using his ability to rouse her senses as a form of persuasion as he had used it last year to trick her into marrying him. Now he was trying to trick her into staying married to him.

'But Solange said you were still in love with her and that you'd visited her several times since she returned,' she said coolly.

'She was lying, God knows why,' he said with a touch of bitterness.

'You have to agree that it's not easy for me to know which of you has told the truth,' she complained. 'She said one thing and you're saying another. You could be lying too.'

His breath hissed furiously as he drew it in. His hands gripped her upper arms and he shook her violently, so that her head wagged back and forth like a rag doll's.

'Why should I lie to you, tell me that?' he demanded angrily, his face close to hers. She could hear his heart pounding with the explosion of his anger.

'Yvan, please, let go of me,' she gasped, afraid of what he might do in anger. She tried to wriggle free, but he leaned his weight across her body, pinning her down against the bed and encircling her throat with one hand.

'No, you're not going to run away again,' he muttered. 'You're going to tell me what you believe I'd gain by lying to you about Solange.'

'You ... you've said yourself that you want to keep our marriage intact,' she whispered shakily, wondering if he had any idea of how strong his fingers were and that they were in danger of cutting off her breath for ever. The weight of his body lying on hers was a familiar warmth to which her own body was beginning to respond in spite of her efforts to keep it under control.

'What's wrong with that?' he exclaimed. 'I make an explanation which I could have made last year if you'd let me. I tell you the truth and you don't believe me. Why? Why?'

His fingers flexed about her throat, but now their touch was more subtly dangerous; now they caressed her skin slowly, sending shivers of exquisite pleasure through her body.

'Because you know what's in my uncle's will,' she accused. 'You married me because he bribed you to!'

'*Zut*, you suffer from delusions, *ma mie*,' he scoffed softly, and his lips touched the hollow of her throat. She smelt the strange earthy smell of his hair as it brushed against her face, and squeezing her eyes shut and clenching her fists she willed herself not to respond to the touch of his coaxing fingers and lips. 'How your heart leaps,' he murmured. 'You're frightened, and you had need to be just now. Women have been strangled for less than not trusting their husbands. But let me tell you something: you don't want to believe me because you want an excuse to end our marriage. You ran away last year because you'd discovered you didn't like being married to me, and Solange's lies about me provided the excuse to go back to England to be near a man called Gerald. You knew him before you met me, didn't you?'

To her relief he had sat up. With one arm he bridged her body to support himself as he leaned back so he could look down at her where she lay against the pillow, every expression of her face revealed in the shaft of moonlight which now slanted across the bed. But his fingers stayed at her throat, sliding downwards insidiously to her breast so that she was forced to try and push them away, and instead found her own fingers caught by his and held tightly.

'Yes, I did know Gerald before I met you. He works for Charles. Since his divorce he's often come to Ashleigh. He ... he often invites me to go sailing with him, to play tennis, to go to concerts.'

'He sounds like a fine cultured Englishman,' he remarked with a touch of mockery. 'And he's more to your taste perhaps than a rough French vine-grower. You compared us and he showed up better than I did, so you deserted me in the hope that I'd agree to divorce you.'

'No, oh no, that isn't why I left,' she replied, realising that he had seized the advantage again and instead of admitting he had been in the wrong was blaming her. 'I didn't leave you because of Gerald.'

'Then why did you leave?' he demanded roughly. 'Why did you go away without coming to me first? For God's sake, Elaine, can't you give me one good sensible reason why you ran away without giving me a chance to explain?'

She pulled her hand free from his and with her other covered her face so he couldn't see the remembered pain expressed on her face; that raw slashing pain she had felt in Solange's apartment; the pain of disillusion and destroyed trust.

'I don't know. I can't tell you,' she wailed. 'Oh, Yvan, please don't do that.' Her hands left her face quickly and went to his which was at the bodice of her nightgown flicking undone the tiny buttons. 'Please ... I don't want to ... I can't.'

'But you like it, *chérie,* you know you do,' he whispered, smoothing the dark chiffon away from her body. '*Ah, comme tu es blanche au claire de la lune, blanche et froide comme la neige.*'

'Let me go,' she moaned, twisting away from him, knowing that her resistance to the tender caresses of his hands was failing dismally and that her body was springing to life, passionate joyous life.

Once again he caught and held her, and lay down beside her to gather her against him and hold her close.

'Then it's only since you've been away from me that you've wanted this Gerald,' he suggested wickedly, 'because you have missed this, and this and this.'

Because she felt her body leap in response to his touch she writhed, trying to escape from his seeking fingers.

'I don't want him!' she cried. 'Oh, I don't know what I want,' she groaned helplessly.

'But I do, *chérie.*' Yvan's laughter, muffled in the thickness of her hair, was triumphant, so that once again indignation at his arrogant assumption that he had only to exert his expertise as a lover to make her capitulate flared up inside her.

'Let me go!' she fumed, beating at his shoulders with her fists. 'I don't want to sleep with you. I hate you! I want to sleep in the other room.'

'No, you don't. You'll be lonely there and cold. You are cold too, even though the night is warm. Hate has frozen you up. You're like a little icicle. Let me warm you, melt you.'

'Yvan, please don't ...' Her protest was cut off because his mouth covered hers, and silenced by that hard bruising kiss, she agreed with him that she didn't want to be lonely and cold any more.

At first she responded shyly to his kiss, then clung hungrily to him, lifting her arms to slide her hands over him, stroking him, seeking to rouse his passion as he was rousing hers, feeling the pressure building up inside him while all the cravings of the last nine months gathered together within her. His warmth against her was like fire against ice, cracking it open. Then his warmth was within her and she was melting at last, not caring where she was, knowing only that she was with him again and their union was releasing her from the deep freeze condition in which she had existed since she ran away from him.

When it was over the pleasure and satisfaction which their union had brought to her remained as a memory in the delicious warmth and ease which spread through her body, and blotted from her mind temporarily her suspicions concerning him. No longer lonely and cold, she curled against him gratefully and felt his lips visit her skin, exploring gently until they found her mouth again.

They slept at last, entwined with each other among the tangle of the sheets, the quilt and their two articles of clothing having long since slipped from the bed to the floor. Elaine slept the longest and didn't wake until she felt a cool hand touch her bare shoulder. Opening her eyes, she saw that the room was full of dawn light, pearly grey suffused with rose as the rays of the rising sun spread above the horizon.

Memory of what had happened during the night thrust through the mists of sleep which clogged her mind, yet she was aware of coolness in the bed even though someone had placed the quilt over her.

'Elaine, wake up.' The voice wasn't Yvan's, it was Marguerite's, and the cool hand which touched her bare shoulder again was slender with age. She turned abruptly on to her back and found that she was alone in bed and that Marguerite, fully dressed, was standing beside it.

'Oh! Where's Yvan?' Elaine exclaimed, sitting up and clutching the quilt to her nakedness, and expressing her immediate concern. He had gone without waking her.

'I had to wake him earlier, to send him for Père Gosselin,' explained Marguerite gently. Her face looked more lined than ever and weariness had put blue smudges under her eyes.

Père Gosselin was the parish priest and the fact that Marguerite had had to send for him meant only one thing; Armand's condition had deteriorated during the night so much that he had received the last rites according to his faith.

'Then is Uncle worse?' asked Elaine in a whisper.

'I have to tell you, *chérie,* that he passed away peacefully a few minutes ago.' Marguerite's eyes were calm and tearless. 'Don't grieve too much. He wouldn't have wanted that. For him death came as a great release and you came back in time to make him a little happier. Perhaps you'll get up now and come downstairs for your breakfast? Marie goes to her home for Sunday and I don't like to give Berthe and Jacques too much to do on their day of rest. I'll need your help, *chérie*. There are all the arrangements for the funeral to be made.'

'Oh, don't worry, Tante, I'll help you,' said Elaine impulsively.

'Thank you, *chérie*. I knew I could count on you when the time came.'

As soon as the door closed after Marguerite, Elaine leapt from the bed. After visiting the bathroom she returned to dress quickly in a neat white blouse and a wrap-round skirt of navy blue denim. While she was tying her hair back she stood at the window looking out.

The morning smelt of autumn, she thought, and dew clung sparkling to the creeper and turned each spider-web into a cluster of tiny diamonds. There were a few fallen leaves in the courtyard damp and glistening against the ancient flagstones, and she knew from past experience that moist mushrooms would be poking through the moss in the woods. Last year, on such a Sunday morning, she and Yvan had met at sun-up in the courtyard to go searching for golden-pink chanterelle mushrooms, and by the time they returned in the late afternoon she had promised to marry him.

A movement down in the courtyard drew her attention. The priest in his black soutane and round black hat had appeared, and with him was Yvan. They were on their way to the grey Citroën which was parked by the lily pond.

At the sight of Yvan Elaine's heart jumped and began to kick against her ribs. Her hand went involuntarily to her throat and she felt the pulse beating there too fast. *You are frightened,* he had jeered last night when his fingers had circled about her throat.

Shaken by the memories of all that had happened in this room, above all by the memories of the tender violence of his lovemaking, she watched him see the priest into the front seat of the car and then walk round to the other side of the vehicle so that he was facing the window where she was standing. He paused there for a moment, obviously searching for car keys in the pocket of his denim working trousers, and as she watched the top of his ruffled grey-streaked black hair Elaine played a little fanciful game with herself.

He brought the keys out of his pocket, opened the door, paused and looked across the yard in the direction of the tower doorway. Elaine held her breath, almost willing him to look higher and see her at the window, hardly believing it when he said something to someone who was at the doorway and then ducked into the driver's seat and slammed the car door shut without having even lifted his glance halfway up to the window.

Disappointed, Elaine turned into the room. The sight of her black nightgown, limp and slightly bedraggled on the floor, triggered off an explosion of shamed anger within her because once again Yvan had found it easy to seduce her and had set out deliberately to do so last night, hoping that by making her feel loved and wanted on the physical level he would obliterate her suspicions about him.

Why, oh, why had she let him do it? she raged silently at herself as she snatched up the nightgown from the floor and bundled it into a drawer as if she couldn't bear the sight of it. Why had she let happen the very thing she had wanted to avoid happening? It hadn't resolved anything. Oh, it was true he had explained away the presence of his gloves and lighter in

Solange's apartment, but she still had this suspicion that he had made the explanation to keep their marriage intact, primarily because only as her husband could he inherit any of Chambourtin.

Moving quickly, as if by hurrying she could stop thinking, she plumped the pillows, straightened the sheets and covered the bed with the quilt, then left the room where she had surrendered not to Yvan but to the weakness of her own body, and went downstairs to the kitchen where a glum and silent Jacques served her breakfast.

After the meal she found Marguerite in the study, writing out a list of names of people who would have to be informed of Armand's death and who would probably attend the funeral.

'It's to be very simple. He asked specifically for that, and there are to be no flowers, so tell everyone that,' she instructed after handing over the list of names and telephone numbers. 'I have already contacted the undertaker who has kindly consented to come this morning. You must try and get in touch with Émile Léger, Armand's lawyer, about the will, because he has all the copies of it at his office.' Marguerite sighed as she rose to her feet. 'I'm afraid a Sunday in August isn't the best day to die.'

Two and a half hours later, after making over twelve telephone calls and drawn several blanks because the people she was calling weren't at home, Elaine was inclined to agree with Marguerite; Sunday wasn't a good day on which to die. Leaning on the desk and propping her chin on her hands, she looked out of the window. Beyond the balustrade of the stone terrace she could see the river, shining and serene between its green banks. It was midday. High in the sky the sun had sucked up the dew which had earlier spangled the webs of the spiders and its heat would be rotting the mushrooms in the woods. Calm, windless and cloudless, the day was like the previous one and the one before that, giving the impression that August would last for ever.

'Come and have some lunch, *chérie*.' Marguerite's white head appeared round the edge of the door.

'Oh, yes, please,' said Elaine, and got up from the chair and stretching her arms above her head. 'I'd no idea telephoning could be so tiring. So many people are out too. But who can blame them? It's such a gorgeous day.'

'And I expect you're wishing you could be out too, walking in the woods,' replied Marguerite as they went along to the dining room. 'Perhaps you'll find time later this afternoon.'

The table was set for two only, Elaine noticed as she took her seat, and she wondered for the umpteenth time that morning where Yvan was.

'Isn't Yvan lunching with us?' she asked, hoping that the slight sharpness in her voice didn't betray her uncertainty where he was concerned.

'*Mais non*,' said Marguerite smoothly as she shook out her serviette and placed it on her knee while Jacques set a bowl of cucumber soup in front of her. 'He has gone to Bellevigne. Didn't he tell you?'

Bellevigne, Elaine knew, was the Durocher property, that small yet prosperous vineyard about fifty kilometres to the east, nearer to Angoulême. She knew also that Yvan had inherited his father's share of it and had worked there for a while with his cousin Guy before he had taken over Jean Durocher's job at Chambourtin.

'No, he didn't,' she replied as coolly as she could. 'Did he say when he'd be back?'

'On Tuesday morning. It's a busy time now, as you know, on the land, for soon the *vendange* will be upon us. If you hadn't been here I know he would have stayed to help me today, but you are here and he felt free to go and attend to his own business.'

Elaine frowned as she laid down her soup spoon and the ever-attentive Jacques moved forward to take her bowl and put in its place a plate of delicious-looking ham. There was some mystery which had to be solved and she wasn't quite sure how to solve it without betraying that she knew nothing about Yvan's business. In the end she decided she might as well be honest.

'Tante Marguerite, I'm afraid I don't understand,' she said diffidently. 'What business does Yvan have at Bellevigne? I thought that his cousin Guy looked after it.'

'Not any more. Guy was never very interested in growing vines, you know, and of course he didn't have Yvan's college training in viticulture. Last spring Yvan was able to buy him out, using the money he had saved from working here at Chambourtin. He now owns all of Bellevigne and has lived there for the past six months.' Marguerite spoke smoothly still, as if she saw nothing strange in having to explain to her son's wife what he had been doing for the past six months.

'Oh, I didn't know,' said Elaine weakly, remembering suddenly Yvan's jeer that there was a lot she didn't know. 'He didn't tell me.'

'Perhaps he thought you wouldn't be interested,' said Marguerite coldly. 'When I suggested to him this morning that he should take you to Bellevigne with him he told me that your reconciliation with him had been a pretence only to make Armand happy, and that it had ended with Armand's death. I have to thank you, *ma chère,* for backing me up in my little white lie. I know it helped him to die in peace.'

Feeling dismay shiver through her like a chill, Elaine struggled to copy her companion's smooth civilised behaviour and continued to eat her ham and salad as if she were enjoying every mouthful when in reality they were suddenly tasteless. How had she been so foolish as to have forgotten the pretence?

'It was the least I could do for him,' she explained politely, but she was still puzzled. Yesterday when he had been riding about Chambourtin Yvan had behaved as if he were still manager of the vineyard, or so it had seemed to her. 'Doesn't Yvan work for my . . . I mean, doesn't he work at Chambourtin any more?'

'No, he left the company last March when his contract with them expired. Paul Sevigny took his place. You haven't met him yet?'

'No, I haven't.'

'He's a very pleasant young man. He and his wife Annette live in the cottage where Jean and I used to live. They have two little children. Yvan, of course, still takes an interest in the place, and when he visits me he likes to ride around and have a look at the vines just as he used to do. My dear, you're looking very puzzled.'

'I am,' admitted Elaine miserably. 'You mentioned a company. What company?'

'The St Vérain Company, of course, which owns Chambourtin and the distillery in Cognac.'

'But I thought Uncle Armand owned Chambourtin!'

'Only in so far as he was a shareholder in the company. It was formed at that time I was telling you about, when the vines were failing and the industry was going into a decline; when Armand realised it was too much of a task for him alone to resurrect the place. The company was formed to run the whole operation from the planting of the seeds, the growing and pruning of vines, the harvesting of the grapes to the distilling of the wine, the fermenting of it in oak barrels and the bottling and labelling of it. That company is now under the managing directorship of Michel Morais, one of the people I asked you to phone.'

'I see,' said Elaine, in a low voice. 'I didn't know. You must think I'm very foolish for not knowing.'

'Not really,' said Marguerite gently. 'You are still very young and possibly not very concerned with the complications of the business world. And then the fact that you didn't know is in a way the fault of Armand. He would much rather talk to you about art and music, and re-tell in his own fashion the tales of romance and chivalry. He was also not very concerned with the business of making brandy for a profit, and that was why he let the vineyard be taken over. It was the house that he loved, and he spent every penny he had on it. In fact I wouldn't be at all surprised if when his will is read, we'll find that he was in debt and that there isn't very much for anyone to inherit. Did you manage to get in touch with Emile Léger?'

'No, I haven't, not yet,' replied Elaine in a stifled voice. 'If there isn't much for anyone to inherit, Tante Marguerite, what are you going to do?'

'I have it all planned,' replied Marguerite cheerfully. 'I am going back to La Rochelle, where I was born. I love the sea and all these years I have lived inland I have missed it. I don't expect anything from Armand's will. Jean left me well provided for and I shall take an apartment overlooking the old harbour where I can watch the sailing boats come in and go out, and I shall be near Paulette, my eldest daughter. And I hope that sometimes, Elaine, you will come and visit me there.'

'Thank you, I'd like to.' Elaine mumbled, conscious of desolation beginning to spread through her like a cold blighting wind, noticing that Marguerite had said 'hoped'. She didn't expect to be visited, as a mother-in-law might expect to be visited by her son's wife. And she hadn't included Yvan in the invitation.

'If you'll excuse me now, I'd like to go and have a little nap,' said Marguerite, rising to her feet. 'I didn't have much sleep last night again. Can you manage the rest of the phone calls?'

'Yes.'

Marguerite nodded. '*Eh bien,* don't stay in all afternoon. You're still looking pale.'

CHAPTER SIX

GOING back to the study, Elaine once again applied herself to the task of phoning everyone on Marguerite's list, but after making three calls she found she wasn't concentrating and had no idea whether the people she had contacted were coming to the funeral or not, because she hadn't listened properly to what they had said.

Her mind was too full of what she had learned from Marguerite at lunchtime. She wanted to be quiet somewhere, to sit and think of what the new knowledge meant and how it affected her.

She jumped up from the chair in her usual impulsive way and stepped through the open french window on to the terrace, and leaned for a moment on the balustrade looking down the sweep of the green lawns and woodland to the river. The air was warm and heavy and thick woolly cumulus clouds were building up on the curving horizon.

It would be cooler in the woods, she thought, shady and silent. One leaping vault and she was over the balustrade and down on the firm grass that sparkled with drops of water shed on it by the twirling sprinklers. Soon she was under the shade of spreading oak trees, which were grown specially to produce the casks in which the brandy was stored for five years to mature. It was the staves of oak wood that gave the liqueur its pale golden tint.

At least she knew that much, thought Elaine ruefully, even if she hadn't known that these woods, the great vineyard and the fine modern *chais* in Cognac where the brandy was distilled and stored hadn't belonged solely to her uncle Armand but were owned by a company in which he had been one of the shareholders.

There's a lot you don't know. Yvan's jeer returned to mock. *And when you don't know something instead of asking about it ... you make wild guesses and believe they are the truth. You never cared enough to ask.* The rest of his criticism beat through her mind over and over again.

She hadn't cared enough to ask, it was true, but not in the way he meant. She hadn't cared what he did for a living, she hadn't cared about money or ambitions or inheritances. She hadn't wanted to know about them, had never given them a thought until that day in Solange's apartment. And then she had been so hurt by the evidence, as she had believed, of his infidelity that she had run away rather than ask.

Her reaction had been that of an adolescent rather than an adult. She had behaved as Yvan had said, like a spoilt brat, because something had touched her self-esteem. She hadn't been able to take the possible destruction of the dream of romance which she had woven about her relationship with him, and in which she had starred as the only woman he had ever loved. And she had refused him the chance to explain.

Well, he had had his hearing last night, she thought, sinking down on the trunk of a fallen tree which formed a seat in a glade where sunlight filtered through the leaves, and at the same time he had asserted his rights as her husband, and made the most of the close contact in which their pretend-reconciliation had placed them.

Hot suddenly, not with walking but with the remembrance of the passion which had erupted between them the previous night, Elaine hid her face in her hands. Here in this very wood last summer Yvan had made love to her in a similar way and she had learned for the first time in her life what it was to want a man, and had pleaded with him to take her. To her surprise he had withdrawn at once, twisting away from her to sit up with his back to her to hold his head in his hands much as she was holding hers now.

'I can't,' he had said.

'You mean ... you don't like me enough?' she had said, and he had turned to look at her over his shoulder for a long moment before leaning back on one elbow beside her and lifting a strand of her curling hair to twist it round his fingers.

'No, I don't mean that. I mean that I can't until we're married.'

She had scarcely believed it. Deep in her heart she had always hoped that one day some man might care enough to want to marry her before he wanted to sleep with her, but she hadn't believed that it would be this man; the first she had loved, the first she had ever wanted physically, the first to show her how beautiful passion could be.

She had stared up at his taut dark face for a moment and then joy had been too much for her, and she flung herself against him. Knocked off balance, he had lain back against the soft moss and held her between his two hands as she lay on top of him, and had laughed at her.

'Honestly, Yvan?' she had asked in English.

'Honestly, Elaine,' he had replied in the same language. 'Why do you doubt me?' he had added in French.

Because she found herself for once in a commanding

position she had studied his face, tracing an eyebrow with the point of one finger, sliding the same finger down the straight line of his nose to press it against his mouth.

'Well, I know that you've had lots of girl-friends,' she said.

'Do you? Who told you that?'

'Jeanne Sorel.' Jeanne had been the housemaid at the chateau last summer.

'So you discuss me with the maid,' he had growled at her with mock ferocity.

'No. But she likes to talk about you. She has a crush on you,' she had replied, pleased to have something about which she could tease him as he often teased her. 'You're very handsome, you know, *mon ami,* and you have that *je ne sais quoi* which attracts women.'

'And teenage housemaids,' he murmured dryly. 'But tell me why the fact that I've had many girl-friends makes you doubt that I want to marry you?'

Elaine flushed. 'I'm not very pretty and ... and I've no real experience ... I mean, I've never been sexually involved with a man before ... and I don't know much about making love.' Her voice had faded to a whisper and she had buried her suddenly hot face against his shoulder.

He was silent for a while, stroking her hair. Then, both hands at her waist, he had pushed her off him on to her back against the soft cushioning moss and leaned over her.

'For me you are very pretty with your golden hair and your white skin and your pansy-dark eyes,' he had said gently. 'As for the rest,' he shrugged his shoulders, 'I think I'm glad there has been no one before me. Perhaps you should know, *ma petite,* that none of the women I've known can compare with you in any way, and that's why I'm asking you to marry me. But why are you crying, *ma mie*? Have I hurt you in some way?'

'No, oh no. It's just that I'm so happy.' She had put her arms round her neck and pulled his face down close to her. A shiver of ecstasy went through her as he had licked the teardrops which dripped off her lashes and slid down her cheeks before his lips had claimed hers.

'*Eh bien,* if you are happy then so am I,' he had said a few minutes later as he helped her to her feet, and with their arms around each other they had wandered slowly back through the woods to the chateau.

Armand had been delighted with the news. Marguerite, Elaine remembered now, had been more reserved. It had been at Armand's insistence that they had been married in church, although Elaine hadn't cared one way or the other where or how she had been married. All she had wanted was to be with Yvan, to know he was hers. Her love had been totally possessive and selfish, she could see that now. It had blinded her to what had been going on around her and she had never noticed until that rude awakening in Solange's apartment that Yvan had never told her that he loved her.

He hadn't told her last night either. For him marriage was a convenience, an arrangement which gave him certain rights which he had no hesitation in claiming when the opportunity offered, as it had last night when he had found her in the bed where she had said he could sleep.

Oh, she didn't deny that she had wanted him and that their union had brought to her the same joyous pleasure that it had brought when they had first been married, but there was still this niggling suspicion that he had been using their relationship deliberately to distract her and she . . . she, so lonely and cold, had let herself be distracted and had made believe that their reconciliation was real and not just pretence.

It had all turned out very differently from what she had expected when she had left London on Friday morning. Then she had thought she had sufficient strength of will to resist being dominated by him. Now she realised that instinctively she had known that any meeting with him would be dangerous for her, and that was really why she had stayed away from him for nine months. He possessed her in the way that devils sometimes possessed people. *Better the devil you know than the devil you don't,* he had said when they had met on Friday, meaning she would be better off staying married to him than she would be getting a divorce and marrying someone else.

She stood up and began to walk back along the path which tunnelled under the green-fringed branches of the oak trees, head down, hands in the patch pockets of her denim skirt, and the brassy colour of her hair occasionally gleaming like gold when a stray sunbeam filtering through the leaves touched it.

She didn't really want to marry anyone else, Elaine thought. In comparison with Yvan, Gerald meant nothing. She didn't even care that Gerald had invited Lucy to go cruising with him this weekend. But she did care if Yvan was involved with another woman—she cared with a furious passionate jealousy which even now was making her hands curl in her pockets.

And that was the problem. Could she stay married to Yvan knowing that there might always be someone like Solange hovering in the background and knowing that he wasn't prepared to tell her everything about himself? Knowing that he had married her not because he loved her, but because her uncle had arranged the marriage in the old French style in the hope of making his own crazy dream of a child come true?

A child! Elaine stopped suddenly and her hands went to her stomach, the fingers spreading fanwise across its flatness as if she expected to feel a swelling there within her womb. Heart thudding, her mouth dry with a strange elated sort of panic, she stood there in the leaf-dappled, mould-scented silence of the woods.

Last night no precautions had been taken. There had been no time, no thought given to any consequences of their union. They had come together explosively because they had wanted each other. They had behaved as if they loved each other, so it was possible she would have a child.

Unable to bear the strain of her thoughts any longer, she began to run along the leaf-matted path and emerged at last from the green solitude of the woods into the brightness of hot sunlight. Her breast heaving, her skin sticky with sweat, she tried to recover her breath as she walked across the lawn and up the steps to the terrace. From the study came the sound of the telephone ringing. She raced along the terrace, flung herself through the french window and across to the desk, lifted the receiver and just managed to find breath to speak into it.

'Ah, *bonjour*, Madame Durocher. Emile Léger here,' said a cool crisp masculine voice. 'I'm sorry to hear of Monsieur St Vérain's death. I believe you were trying to contact me earlier.'

'Yes. My mother-in-law Madame St Vérain suggested I should, because you have all the copies of my great-uncle's will.'

'That is so. I've a copy here beside me, *madame*, and

although it isn't my usual custom to read a will over the phone I expect you'd like to know if he left any special instructions concerning his burial?'

'Er ... yes ... please,' agreed Elaine.

'Normally I would drive over to Chambourtin to do this, but since it's Sunday and we have weekend guests staying with us, I hope you'll excuse me this once. I'll be over tomorrow morning when I hope Madame St Vérain, your husband, yourself and members of the household staff will be present, because you are all beneficiaries under the will. He asked to be buried in the St Vérain vault in the churchyard at St Augustine's. No flowers by request and just a small reception afterwards when everyone who attends is to be served a glass of St Vérain brandy. There, that is all. Seems straightforward. What time would be convenient for me to call on you in the morning, *madame*?'

'Eleven o'clock?' suggested Elaine tentatively.

'Excellent! That is very suitable for me. It won't take long—Monsieur St Vérain had very little to leave since everything is owned by the company now, and ... I beg your pardon? Did you say something?'

'I asked if the company also owned the chateau?'

'Yes, although it isn't common knowledge. Monsieur St Vérain didn't like it to be known that he couldn't afford the upkeep of it any more. The company let him live there as its caretaker, you might say, because of course it is an exquisite example of the chateau architecture and has I believe many historical associations. But of late your great-uncle became slightly confused in his mind and seemed to think that it was still his to bequeath. He wanted very much to add a codicil to his will leaving the chateau in trust to the children of your marriage to Monsieur Durocher. I had the greatest difficulty with him over this matter.'

'Do you mean the codicil was never added?' asked Elaine.

'That is correct, *madame*. There was no point, you see, since he no longer owned the chateau. All he had to leave were his few shares in the company, some pieces of furniture and *bric-à-brac*. But you shall hear all tomorrow. *Au revoir, madame*.'

'Au revoir.'

Elaine let the receiver clatter down on the rest and stood for a moment clutching her head with her hands. No wonder Marguerite had said she suspected that Armand had very little to leave in his will, and might even be in debt.

A sudden urge to talk with Yvan again came over her. She flicked through the small book beside the phone which contained the phone numbers of family and friends, thinking to find the number for Bellevigne. There wasn't one. Throwing the book aside, she heaved out the local phone directory and went through the Durochers. None seemed to live at Bellevigne.

Outside the study she hesitated in the hall wondering whom to ask for the number, and decided to ask Jacques rather than disturb Marguerite. She found him sitting in an old deck chair in the courtyard a newspaper over his face as he snoozed.

He jumped when she spoke to him, removed the newspaper and blinked at her.

'Now what can I do to help you, *madame*?' he asked politely.

'Can you tell me the phone number at Bellevigne?'

'No, *madame*, because there is no phone there yet. Monsieur Yvan hasn't been able to get one installed yet.'

'Oh, what a nuisance! I have to get in touch with

him. He's supposed to be here in the morning when the lawyer comes.'

'Then may I suggest you drive there, in Monsieur St Vérain's car. I have the keys in the kitchen.'

'But I'm not sure where Bellevigne is,' Elaine said cautiously.

'Go back along the road as if you were going to Chambourtin village, but instead of crossing the bridge follow the dirt road which runs beside the river on this side. It's a rough ride, but it's more direct than going right back to the Route Nationale and south again. After you've gone several kilometres you'll come to a narrow made road which angles inland away from the river. Bellevigne is along that road, past the village of Bellic.'

'How will I recognise it?' she asked.

'It is a pretty white house set back from the road among a clump of cypress trees. I believe the name Durocher is on the post box at the end of the lane leading to it. Shall I get the keys, *madame*?'

'Yes, please.'

The car was the same one that she had driven last year to Poitiers, a dark blue Peugeot a little the worse for wear. As she drove it away through the archway between the two old *chais,* Elaine felt again as if she were running away. Only this time she was running away from Chambourtin to see her husband.

It was a good idea to go and see where he lived, she thought, and maybe they would be able to talk more satisfactorily now that she knew so much more. Maybe she would be able to find out the answers to the questions which were plaguing her. If there was nothing much for her to inherit except possibly a few shares in the St Vérain company, why had Yvan married her? It could hardly have been to better himself, as Solange had suggested, because he was already a man of property himself and owned a vineyard half of which he had purchased with the money he had saved.

But why should she believe any more anything that Solange had said? Considering what she had learned since she had returned to Chambourtin everything the woman had told her was suspect, because she had been wrong about Marguerite, she had been wrong about the ownership of Chambourtin, and so had probably been wrong about Yvan's reason for marrying Elaine Cooper.

Realising that she was heading for the bridge that crossed the river, Elaine braked and looked for the opening to the dirt road that Jacques had mentioned. It was there to the right, more a wide continuation of the towpath than a road, and only wide enough for one car, but the hot dry summer had given its surface a hardness which made it fairly easy to drive along, although here and there she bumped down into a pot-hole and the springs of the Peugeot protested noisily.

At last she reached the junction with the road which angled inland from the river and turned on to it. It had a fairly good surface and was dead straight, edged by the usual poplars. On either side fields of ripening grain alternated with terraces of vines. She passed by a huddle of pastel-coloured buildings and a church tower hiding among cypress and poplars which called itself Bellic, and began to look for a small white house set back from the road, driving slowly along the road, which was fairly free of traffic, and watching for a post box at the end of a lane with the name of Durocher on it.

She was passing a field of cabbages out of which the ruins of an old stone abbey with delicately pillared apse and a weathered red-tiled roof seemed to grow, when to her surprise the car seemed to stop. She pressed down on the accelerator and it jerked forward, stopped, jerked again. A quick glance at the petrol gauge showed her that the needle was pointing to empty, so using the small amount of momentum she guided the vehicle into the side of the road, and switched off the ignition.

For a moment she sat there wanting to laugh. How like her to set off without a thought about whether there was enough petrol in the tank to last her the whole journey! The nearest petrol pumps were probably in the village that she had passed through about two kilometres back along the road. But she was sure she couldn't be far from Bellevigne now, so it would make more sense to set off and walk there.

It wasn't until she was out of the car and locking the doors that Elaine realised how the weather had changed. Those big clouds she had seen forming earlier were now pushing up into a big grey mushroom which was attempting to obscure the sun, although in the area where she was the fields still shimmered under bright yellow light.

Walking would have been pleasant if the air hadn't been so hot and humid, and she was glad of the shade cast by a line of poplars. It was very still and very quiet and as far as she could see there was no habitation, just rows and rows of vines on either side, drooping from the wires along which they were trained with the weight of the ripening grapes.

Then she heard it, the rumble of thunder. Looking back, she saw that a big dark cloud with a lining of ugly orange light was spreading over the sun. It looked very much as if it were going to catch up with her, and she was going to be caught in the storm.

She had just reached the end of a narrow lane where

a green wooden box with the name Durocher painted on it in white letters was attached to a wooden post when the thunder rumbled again and raindrops, big and hard, began to rattle on the dry road and to hit her bare arms and head. Holding her handbag over her hair in an attempt to keep it dry, she turned into the lane and began to run, seeing far ahead of her the glimmer of white walls among the spear-like shapes of green cypresses.

The way was uphill and she had to slow down to a walk several times to catch her breath. Above her lightning crackled and more thunder growled. Rain was falling so heavily that the streams of water were beginning to rush down the sides of the lane and by the time Elaine reached a courtyard full of puddles her clothing and her hair were soaked and her feet were squelching in her flat-heeled open sandals.

She saw a door which had a small tiled roof over it and dashed towards it to wait under the shelter while she regained her breath, noticing the grey Citroën parked in front of the open doorway of a stone outbuilding. The sight of the car was reassuring. Yvan must be either in the house or somewhere on the land among the vines.

Turning, she looked at the door. It was old, made from strips of wood, and had a latch which lifted. She knocked. No one came. She lifted the latch, pulled the door open and stepped into a wide stone-walled, stone-floored passage.

'Yvan!' she called, and walked along the passage, hearing the sound of water gushing from a tap. The noise seemed to be coming from a doorway on the right.

When she reached the doorway she looked through the open door into a big room which was obviously a kitchen. Big oak beams crossed its ceiling and from them hung strings of golden onions, dried herbs and some smoked hams. The stone walls were painted cream and one of them was taken up by a huge hearth. Set at right angles to the hearth were two old settles, their wood dark and polished with use. On a long wooden table, the top of which had been scoured white with many scrubbings, were the remains of a meal: the half of a long crusty loaf, a crock of butter, a board with a yellow cheese on it, a dirty plate and knife, a green wine bottle and pieces of broken glass which had once been a wine glass. Near the pieces was a small pool of red wine.

For a moment Elaine stood, her gaze transfixed by the broken glass and the pool of wine. Then she looked over to the window which was set into the thick stone wall. Under it was the sink where Yvan stood, oblivious to her presence, holding his hand under the water which gushed noisily from a tap. His hair was tousled as if he had been out in a high wind and he was swearing to himself, slowly and succinctly.

'Oh, what have you done to yourself?' she demanded, running across the room to his side, and suddenly feeling a little faint when she saw the gash in his hand. It angled across the loose skin between the lower end of his thumb and his palm, a place which someone had once told her it was dangerous to cut.

He jumped in surprise as if he'd been shot, and turned to stare at her in astonishment while the water continued to gush over his hand.

'How the hell did you get here?' he demanded roughly, then clapped his other hand to his forehead. '*Mon dieu,* don't tell me I've started to see things! I haven't drunk that much wine,' he added self-mockingly.

Elaine looked at him closely then, seeing the heaviness of his eyes, the unpleasant set of his mouth, smelling the sweet scent of the wine he had drunk.

'No, you're not seeing things,' she said, realised she was shouting above the sound of the water and leaned over to turn the tap off. 'I'm really here. I came in the Peugeot and walked.'

'Make up your mind,' he jeered, his glance swerving from her to his wounded hand from which the blood had started to well again. 'You can't have driven and walked at the same time.'

'I didn't. I drove first and then I walked. I ran out of petrol...'

'Ha!' His crack of laughter had a demoniac sound and coincided with a livid flash of lightning which lit up the dimness of the room. 'Typical. Typical. You never think,' he mocked.

'Yvan, are you drunk?'

'Perhaps, I am ... a little. This has had a sobering effect,' he explained, pointing to the wound.

Her glance went to the injury. To her it seemed to be a wide gash from which his blood was pouring into the sink; Yvan's life-blood draining away.

'Oh, we must bind it up!' she exclaimed frantically. 'Where's your first aid kit? Have you got bandages? Tell me where they are and I'll get them. We must staunch the blood. Oh, dear God, if we don't you'll die!'

'A lot you'd care if I did,' he jibed nastily.

'Oh, I would. I'd care very much. Yvan, have you no idea where you have bandages or sterile pads and sticking plaster—anything to stop the blood until I can get you to a hospital to have that gash stitched.'

'*N'importe*—it doesn't matter,' he muttered. 'And there are no bandages.'

'But you should have such things. Oh, what shall I do?' Elaine looked round wildly, saw a cotton towel hanging on a rail and snatched at it. It looked clean and was thin with age so she had no trouble ripping a strip from it.

'Hold your hand under the tap again,' she ordered, and reached to turn the tap on. When the blood had been washed away she turned the tap off. 'Now keep still while I wrap this round it.'

It wasn't easy to do, but at last she had a makeshift pad against the wound and had bound it close to Yvan's hand with another strip from the towel.

'You're really very foolish for not having a first aid kit in the house, especially in a place so far away from anywhere as this is. Supposing I hadn't come?' she said.

'Why are you so wet?' Yvan asked quite irrelevantly, and she looked up. He was staring at her with a strange burning expression in his eyes.

'The storm broke when I was walking here. Didn't you hear the thunder?'

'I heard it.' He closed his eyes suddenly and swayed slightly against the sink, catching hold of the edge of it with his good hand to steady himself. '*Mon dieu,* I feel weak!'

'I'm not surprised, considering you've emptied a bottle of wine by yourself and have lost some blood. You'd best sit down. I'll make some coffee and try to find something more suitable for a bandage. Come on, sit here. Does it hurt?' Elaine tried to speak briskly, but at the thought of his being hurt her voice shook.

'It's throbbing,' he muttered, sitting down on one of the settles and supporting his injured hand on his left forearm. 'You should take off those wet clothes and . . .'

'And what do you suggest I should wear instead—

nothing?' she retorted tartly. 'Or do you keep a supply of women's clothes? Perhaps you have some clothes that were left here by one of your girl-friends.'

'That's what's known as hitting a man when he's down,' he grumbled with a slight smile. 'No, I don't have any women's clothing, but you could wear one of my shirts. It would cover most of you. You'll find one in the bedroom above this room. Now go and do as I tell you.'

She had been busy filling the kettle and setting it on the ring on a big gas cooker, finding ground coffee, a coffee pot and a filter before going across to the table to pick up the pieces of glass amd mop up the spilt wine.

'All right, I'll go in a minute,' she said. 'How did you break the glass?'

'I was testing my strength,' he parried with a sardonic grin. 'Are you going to do as I tell you or do I have to take those wet clothes off you myself?'

'Oh, you're so bossy!' she flung at him, and ran from the room.

The stairs leading to the upper floor of the house were narrow and steep, going straight up between two walls. At the top was a passage like the one downstairs and there were two doorways, one of which led into a big room over the kitchen.

The room had one dormer window and its ceiling sloped to follow the shape of the roof of the house. Its stone walls were also painted cream and it was furnished very simply, with a big double bed and two chests of drawers. Rag rugs covered the wooden floor, their colours matching those in the flowered curtains at the window.

She was glad the house was old and had character, thought Elaine, as she slipped off her wet clothes.

Given a free hand she could make it look attractive, she knew she could, and it would be cosier to live in than the chateau at Chambourtin, which was really more like a museum, full of delicate and valuable antiques.

About to take one of Yvan's blue denim shirts from a drawer, she stared down at it, her eyes wide as she realised the direction her thoughts had been taking. What was the matter with her? She wasn't going to live here at Bellevigne, for the simple reason that she had never been asked to come and live here, and had never even been told that Yvan lived here.

But she would like to live here, her thoughts moved on as if she had never checked them. She would like to sleep in that big bed and wake every morning to see the leaves of the old poplar tree twinkling at her through the window. Shaking the shirt out, she pulled it on and began to roll the long sleeves above her elbows while she wandered across to look out the window. She could make a garden out there, and plant red roses so that the scent of them would rise to the open window in the hot summer nights while the nightingale sang to the moon.

She shook her head sharply. She was romanticising again! Better to face facts. Yvan didn't want her here. If he had wanted her to come he would have invited her. The fact that he hadn't told her about his ownership of Bellevigne showed how much he had rejected her.

Elaine gnawed at her lower lip, trying not to let desolation take over as she buttoned the denim shirt. It reached almost to her knees and covered her very adequately, because it was very wide. She went back to the chest of drawers and looked through them for something with which to bandage Yvan's hand, found some handkerchiefs and took two of them. Then taking up her wet skirt and shirt, she draped them over a chair to dry and went downstairs to the kitchen.

Thunder rumbled a little further away this time, but rain was still lashing the kitchen window and the room was dim. The only sound was that of the kettle boiling. She went over to it and poured water into the filter-cup full of coffee which she had placed in the top of the coffee pot and waited for it to drip through, feeling the stone floor chilly against the soles of her bare feet. When the water had dripped through she poured some more in and then turned to look at Yvan.

He seemed to be asleep, his head tilted sideways against the high back of the settle. As she stood in front of him she felt a surge of love for him, a longing to put her arms round him, to smooth back his tousled hair, rub her cheek against his lean and prickly one and perhaps touch his lips with hers, provocatively, invitingly.

Her glance went to his injured hand. No more blood showed through the makeshift bandage, but he looked pale and there was a slight frown between his eyebrows as if he could feel pain even though he was asleep. Sitting down on the settle beside him, she touched his good hand with her fingers. It felt cold to her touch and she leaned forward to look more closely, worried by the coldness of his skin, and thought she had never known him to be cold. Always he was warm, full of vibrating energy.

'Yvan,' she whispered urgently, wishing that she knew more about the shock produced by a wound, wishing she were less fanciful and more practical and that she were the placid organised wife that he needed. 'Yvan, are you all right?'

'Mmm?' He didn't open his eyes or move in any way.

'Your hand, is it hurting badly? Perhaps I should drive you into the hospital to have it stitched.'

'*Non, n'importe,* it doesn't matter,' he muttered. His eyes glimmered at her briefly through his lashes and a faint sardonic smile curved his mouth. 'You could hardly appear at the hospital in Angoulême dressed like that.'

She glanced down at the shirt and agreed with him ruefully. To appear dressed like this on a Sunday in a small provincial hospital would cause raised eyebrows and a certain amount of gossip.

'But I'm worried about you. It looked such a large gash and you're so cold,' she said anxiously.

'It isn't as big as you think. I looked at it while you were upstairs. It's stopped bleeding and I think it will heal satisfactorily without stitches,' he said, and straightened himself up, pushing his hair back with his uninjured hand. 'Some coffee will help. It should be percolated by now. It smells good. Put plenty of sugar in it. You'll find some mugs in the cupboard by the sink.'

He spoke coolly and curtly: any weakness he might be feeling was hidden behind the usual impassivity of his expression. Elaine stared at him for a moment, feeling a strange aching hopelessness rising within her. It was as if yesterday and last night had never been; as if there had been no rose on her breakfast tray put there by him; as if there had been no ride on a bicycle with him; as if there had been no joyous passionate mating in the night.

'The coffee, Elaine,' he prompted quietly, 'that is if you don't mind.'

The irony was like a dagger thrust. She started and

sprang to her feet and rushed over to the range. During the few months she had lived with him at Chambourtin she had never had to do anything for him in the way of making meals or washing clothes, because all that had been done by the small staff of servants. Now his remark seemed to imply that she didn't want to do anything like that for him.

Clamping her lips together to hold back a retort, she felt tears well in her eyes because instead of being closer to each other they seemed to be even further apart. She found the mugs and the sugar and poured the coffee. She noticed the rain was easing a little and the cloud that had brought the storm was drifting away.

She put the mugs on a small tray and carried it over to the settle. She indicated which was for Yvan and he took it in his good hand. Placing the tray on the settle, she sat down beside it, picked up her mug and sipped a little of the hot coffee, trying to remember why she had come to Bellevigne that afternoon.

'Not bad.' Yvan spoke suddenly and set his mug down on the tray. 'For a woman who was brought up in England you make good coffee. I'd like some more, please.'

She glanced at him, half inclined to tell him to go and get it himself because she wasn't a servant, but he wasn't looking at her. He was looking at his bandaged hand and the frown was back between his eyebrows. All at once the urge to do something for him, to help him, came surging back and without a word she stood up and taking his empty mug went over to the cooker.

As she set the full steaming mug back on the tray between them and sat down again she remembered why she had come.

'Yvan, I came over this afternoon because there's something I must know.'

'Couldn't it have waited until Tuesday?' he asked rather wearily. 'I'm coming for the funeral, you know. I'd have seen you again before you went back to England. Or perhaps you've decided not to wait for the funeral? Perhaps now that your uncle is no longer with us and there's no more need for pretence you're going back to London tomorrow as you'd planned.'

No more need for pretence. Elaine's hand shook and she had to put down her mug of coffee. Why did she keep forgetting that was all it had been, a pretence at reconciliation; a pretence which had lasted only one day and not the days or weeks he had suggested it might last on Friday; a pretence to which she had agreed reluctantly, because deep in her heart she had known that it would end with a moment like this when she found herself wishing that it hadn't been pretence at all, but real.

'No, I'm not returning to England tomorrow as I'd planned,' she said, and her voice sounded thin and faint in her own ears. 'I want to be at the funeral, but there won't be much time for us to talk then.'

'I understand,' he said curtly, and rather irritably. 'You want an answer to your request for a divorce. *Eh bien,* I have thought about it and I've decided that it would be for the best to let you go ahead and divorce me.'

The shock was shattering. Elaine knew that she had gone white because her face felt taut and cold. She knew she was staring wide-eyed because her eyes felt strained and dry. Nothing had been further from her mind than the question of a divorce when she had set out from Chambourtin this afternoon.

'On what grounds?' It came out in a crack from an

aching throat and through parched lips, and he gave her a sharp glance before shrugging his shoulders.

'Whatever you like,' he replied, his mouth twisting wryly. 'I should imagine you won't have much difficulty in finding suitable grounds with the help of a good lawyer. You look a little surprised. Were you beginning to think I'd never agree? Or have you changed your mind again?'

Her head bent because she could not bear to face the satirical mockery which she knew would be glinting in his eyes and curving his mouth. She swallowed in an effort to clear her throat before she spoke again.

'Yes, it is a surprise,' she mumbled eventually. 'After last night ...' She couldn't go on because pain and bewilderment were choking her. She longed to spring to her feet and run from the room, escape from this uncomfortable situation. But she had done with running away. Last year it hadn't solved anything; she had to stay and see this through right to the end even though she realised that the end could be bitter.

'What happened last night?' he asked, his voice cool.

She gasped and flung back her head to stare at him. The heavy-lidded eyes returned her gaze. She had hoped to surprise a glint of humour in them, but they were without light, without expression, and his mouth was a straight hard line.

'You know very well what happened. You and I ... we ... we made love,' she said, her voice unsteady with the pain she was feeling because last night had apparently meant so little to him that he had to question her about it.

'Did we?' he drawled, and she flinched at the irony. 'I hadn't realised love came into it. I thought it was just a case of us both needing some sexual satisfaction, and we happened to find ourselves in the same room on the same bed and the rest followed naturally. The fact that we were still married when it happened merely legalised the situation.'

Bewilderment and a sense of furious outrage fused together in Elaine at the implied insult. He was having his revenge for what she had said to him last night. The desire to fling herself at him to hit him or scratch him was strong, but remembering how little it had gained for her on other occasions she clamped her lips together and clenched her hands until the anger had passed.

'Do you really think that . . . that . . . I would let you do what you did last night only because I wanted sexual satisfaction?' she managed to say at last.

'*Mais oui.* It was convenient for both of us and very pleasurable, at least for me. I hope it was for you too,' he replied smoothly.

'But if you think it was pleasurable how can you talk about divorce today?' she exclaimed.

'Because it's what you want, *ma mie.* Don't you remember on Friday you said you hadn't come here to be reconciled with me—that you wanted a divorce and that nothing, not even the possibility of being cut out of your great-uncle's will, would make you change your mind about me? *Et maintenant,* your uncle is dead. There is no danger of hurting his feelings any more or of your being cut out of his will by such an action, so I'm doing what you want, agreeing to a divorce—at last.'

Yvan spoke quietly without any mockery. His head tilted back against the high back of the wooden settle he had closed his eyes again and the frown line had appeared between his eyebrows. Silent and stunned,

Elaine studied his face, seeing for the first time lines about his mouth and under his eyes, a hollowness in his cheeks which told their own story. Marguerite had said she guessed he was unhappy about something. He looked unhappy now, she thought, desperately so, in the way she had been when she had run away last year, and the thought of his unhappiness hurt her as if it were her own so that she had to do something to help ease it.

'But ... is ... is a divorce what *you* want?' she asked tentatively.

He opened his eyes and his sombre glance lingered thoughtfully on her face as she leaned forward hopefully.

'If it will make you happy again it is what I want,' he replied gently. 'To make you happy is all I have ever wanted.'

A ray of pale rain-washed sunlight struggling free from the grey storm cloud glinted in through the window. It reached across the room to gleam on Elaine's drying hair and to warm her pale cheek. And it seemed to her like the ray which was lighting up her mind as she realised the implication of what Yvan had just said.

'Does that mean ...' she began, when another voice interrupted her calling from the passageway. Female and slightly strident, it shouted a greeting.

'*Âllo, âllo* there, Yvan! Where are you hiding? I hope you're at home now that I'm here after driving through the storm. Ah, *quelle tempête*! The rain was terrible.'

Elaine was conscious of going cold, of freezing up again as she recognised the voice. Turning quickly, she looked towards the doorway and stared incredulously.

Solange Bourget, thin and dark, dressed in cream slacks and a cream sleeveless crocheted top with her black hair waving about her bony vital face, stood there, and behind her hovered a tall blond man with a beard.

CHAPTER SEVEN

FOR a few brief moments of silence tension quivered in the room as the two people sitting on the settle stared at the two people in the doorway, managing to convey by their stares their resentment at the interruption.

Then Yvan moved, rising to his feet and thrusting his right hand into his trouser pocket to hide the makeshift bandage.

'*Bonjour,* Solange,' he said, his deep voice smooth. 'I wasn't expecting to see you so soon.'

Solange moved forward, her hands outstretched, her dark face lit up by a dazzling smile. Going right up to Yvan, she held him by the arms and reached forward to touch his cheeks with hers, French fashion.

'Ah, *mon cher ami,*' she said, 'it is good to see you.' She swung round and flung out a hand to the tall man who had followed her into the room. 'Come, Sven,' she added, 'let me introduce you to my very dear friend Yvan Durocher.' The dark deep-set eyes slanted a glance down at Elaine, who was sitting as if turned to ice on the edge of the settle. 'And to his—as I had thought until now—his estranged wife, Elaine,' continued Solange with a touch of wicked mockery.

The tall man, who seemed like a blond giant out of some Viking saga, stepped forward and nodded at Yvan and then at Elaine.

'I'm Sven Bjorling,' he growled. 'I'm glad to meet you both.'

'You're welcome,' said Yvan politely. 'Please sit

down. Elaine, perhaps you would make some more coffee?'

'Yes, yes, of course.' Elaine rose to her feet stiffly, picked up the tray and, very conscious that Solange was regarding the shirt she was wearing and her bare feet with ill-concealed amusement, she went over to the sink, her ears strained to catch what the others were saying.

'When did you return from Paris?' Yvan said.

'Late last night,' replied Solange. 'I'm so sorry I missed you, *mon ami,* and I hope my absence from home didn't inconvenience you in any way. Madame Oulette said you seemed a little disturbed about something, and that's why I thought I'd come over this afternoon to see you.'

As she measured coffee grounds Elaine felt jealousy stab through her. Why was it that everything Solange said always seem to suggest that her relationship with Yvan was intimate?

'No, I wasn't inconvenienced,' Yvan said smoothly. 'Are you on holiday here in France, Monsieur Bjorling?' he added, directing the conversation away from personal issues.

'Not exactly,' replied Sven. 'I am an artist also and I paint wherever I happen to be living.'

'Sven and I met in Stockholm last year,' put in Solange quickly as her companion paused, having difficulty with the language. 'He wrote to me saying he was coming to Paris and would like to see more of France, so I went up to meet him and invited him down here to stay for a while. He hopes to go on to Spain later.'

Now Solange sounded as if she were trying to placate Yvan, thought Elaine; almost as if she didn't want him to think there was anything going on between her and the Scandinavian—as a woman might try to placate a jealous lover when she was discovered by him with another man. As she set the kettle on the stove she glanced sideways at Yvan to see if he looked jealous. Standing in front of the hearth, both hands now in his pockets, he was looking at Solange as she sat on one of the settles. His eyes were narrowed and his mouth had that ugly cynical twist to it. Apparently his thoughts were far from pleasant. Sven was sitting on the other settle looking slightly embarrassed.

'Why did you call on me yesterday?' asked Solange, returning to the personal again and refusing to be sidetracked.

'To collect some of my belongings which I believe I left in your apartment,' said Yvan coolly.

Her cheeks suddenly burning, Elaine busied herself by getting four more mugs out of the cupboard and setting them on the tray.

'Belongings of yours?' Solange's voice had just the right lilt of surprise in it. 'Do I have some belongings of yours?'

'*Mais oui,* have you forgotten?' Mockery rippled through the smoothness of Yvan's voice. 'Last time I visited you—to buy a painting from you one day last December, I believe it was—I left my cigarettes, lighter and gloves on a table in your apartment. Elaine saw them there, later the same day.'

The mugs were set out on the tray. Elaine turned and leaned against the counter by the sink. Across the room her glance met the challenging glance of Solange's eyes.

'Did you, Elaine?' Solange queried. 'Then why didn't you take them with you when you left?'

It was a good question, thought Elaine miserably. Yet how could she possibly answer it now, with a stranger in the room listening and obviously interested, even though he was a little embarrassed by the situation?

'I didn't think,' she muttered, and as she turned back to attend to the coffee she saw the sardonic lift of Yvan's eyebrows as he glanced at her.

'Was that your only reason for calling on me?' Solange's voice was once again soft and seductive.

'*Non.* I had hoped to clear up a little matter which was bothering me,' said Yvan. 'I hoped you'd be able to explain why you told Elaine I had visited you more than once at your apartment in Angoulême.'

'Did she tell you that?' Solange sounded bewildered, and again Elaine turned to face the challenging gleam of the big dark eyes across the room. 'But you must have misunderstood me, Elaine,' continued Solange. Her glance went to Yvan and then returned to Elaine. 'Ah, *mon dieu,*' she whispered, one long thin hand at her throat, 'is that why ... no, surely you didn't think that Yvan and I ...' She didn't finish the sentence, but covered her face with both her hands.

Sven Bjorling looked suddenly worried and leaned forward to say something quietly to Solange, who shook her head and still kept her face covered. Astounded by the woman's reaction and by all it implied, Elaine stood still, feeling frustration boil up within her as she realised that Solange had very cleverly made it look as if she had over-reacted to an imagined situation last December.

She looked at Yvan appealingly. It seemed to her that there was no mercy in the set of his face. Its expression was hard unforgiving.

'I ... I wasn't mistaken,' she said weakly.

Solange looked up, lifting her hair back from her brow with the back of one hand in a gesture which was very familiar. She looked at Yvan and shrugged.

'Why should I lie?' she asked.

'I have wondered,' he replied dryly.

'But you did lie!' It burst out of Elaine suddenly. 'You lied about everything. You said all sorts of things which I've since discovered were untrue. You lied about Yvan's mother when you said she married his father for convenience to be near my uncle. You lied when you suggested that I was going to inherit Chambourtin and that was why Yvan had married me. I know now that Yvan's mother married Jean Durocher before he ever went to work at Chambourtin—I know now that I'm not going to inherit anything very much because Chambourtin is owned by the St Vérain company. And I know now that Yvan visited you only once—that day last December. You lied to me, and I was fool enough to believe everything you said!'

'Elaine, *chérie*, you were over-excited,' Solange spoke softly, almost kindly. 'You imagined it all. I said nothing about Yvan's mother or about Chambourtin, or if I did you misunderstood, easily done when you're using a language which isn't your own, as I'm sure Sven will agree. Perhaps I should say you misinterpreted what I was saying? A word here, a word there would make all the difference. Don't you agree, Yvan?'

'*Mais oui*, that could be,' he said.

Elaine gasped. He was taking Solange's word and not hers! With a strangled cry of protest she turned and ran from the room, much as she had run from Solange's apartment last year. In the passage she paused, realising how scantily she was dressed. She couldn't leave dressed only in this shirt. She would have to put on her damp clothes again, so she ran up the narrow stairs and into the bedroom. The door closed behind her with a crash and she leaned against it for a moment, her head bowed as she tried to control the trembling which had seized her, and she remembered how she had sat in the car in Angoulême nine months ago. Now, as then, she had run away from a situation because she had been unable to deal with it, because she had been hurt by Yvan's association with Solange.

After a while the trembling stopped and a numbness which she recognised took over. Moving like a robot, she began to slip undone the buttons of Yvan's shirt. She pulled it off and threw it on the bed, then picked up her own shirt. It was still quite damp and it felt cold against her bare skin. When it was on she wrapped her denim skirt round her waist. It was patched with damp and slightly creased, but it was her sandals which had suffered the most. They were really sodden.

Still, she would need them if she was going to walk back to Bellic to buy some petrol for the Peugeot so that she could drive back to Chambourtin, she thought, as she sat down on the edge of the bed with her back to the door and began to put one sandal on. A lot of use coming to see Yvan had done! She hadn't said any of the things she had intended to say. She hadn't told him he was expected to be at Chambourtin tomorrow morning for the reading of her uncle's will.

But she had learned that he was willing to go through with a divorce because he wanted her to be happy, and she had hoped or had begun to hope when ... Oh God, if only Solange hadn't come at that moment! But she had, so what was the use in staying?

Tears brimming in her eyes, Elaine pushed the strap which fastened her sandal through the gilt buckle. Because it was wet it was reluctant to go through and she had to jerk it, and all the time her thoughts were racing ahead.

The sooner she was out of this house where she could have been happy the better for her. The sooner she left France the better. Then there would be no more pain and heartbreak. There would be no more joy and pleasure either, she admitted miserably.

When both sandals were on she grabbed up her handbag and tiptoed to the door, opened it as quietly as she could, then started down the stairs. As she stood in the passage she could hear the murmur of voices coming from the kitchen. It sounded very much as if Solange was holding the centre of the stage again. The smell of coffee was an invitation to return to the kitchen, but Elaine turned her back and tiptoed along the passage in the opposite direction to make her way to another door which she presumed was the front door of the house.

That the door wasn't much used was obvious because even when she pressed on the latch and pulled it didn't open at once, so that she had to tug several times and hoped it wouldn't come suddenly and with a clatter. At last it budged, and she flinched as the hinges creaked when it opened. Then she was through and closing it after her.

Out in the rain-washed air she took to her heels and ran down the long narrow road. Birds, refreshed by the rain, were singing happily from the line of poplar trees, and the sky, which was clearing rapidly, was a lovely cool blue. As she reached the end of the road Elaine looked to her left. A car was coming, and spray flew from under its wheels as it passed through the puddles at the side of the road. Hopefully she stepped forward and waved her hand. The car slowed down and came to a stop beside her. She went to the front side window and looked in. The driver was a middle-aged man, plump and dressed in the usual farming denim. As he leaned across to open the door his dark eyes twinkled at her from a broad peasant's face above the thick grey moustache which curled over his top lip.

'*Bonjour, madame*. Can I help you?' he asked.

Quickly Elaine explained her difficulty and asked him for a lift to the petrol station.

'I can do better,' he said, 'I have a spare can of petrol in the boot. We'll pour it into your car's tank. It will be enough to take you to Bellic where you can fill up.'

'*Merci, monsieur*,' she said gratefully, and sat down beside him.

When they reached the Peugeot he was as good as his word, she paid him for the petrol and he went off with a wave. Pleased that so far her getaway had succeeded, Elaine turned the Peugeot round and within a few minutes was at the petrol station at Bellic waiting for the tank to be filled.

Then she was on her way again back to Chambourtin. The road which wound beside the river was not so easy to negotiate because the potholes were now full to the brim with yellowish water, and always as she tried to avoid one she would end up driving into another, so that it took much longer for her to reach the end of the road where the bridge crossed the river into the village of Chambourtin than she had expected.

When she reached the bridge at last she slowed down and guided the car into the side of the road, where she stopped for a few minutes to decide what to do next. She should really turn left and go back to the chateau, to stay there until the will was read and the funeral was over, but it would be easy now to turn right instead and drive to Paris; perhaps catch a plane to England tonight if she were lucky, or at least wait at the airport all night to go aboard the first flight to London in the morning.

Who would be hurt if she didn't go back to Chambourtin? Not her uncle any more. Marguerite might be offended on behalf of Armand, but she wouldn't be surprised. Such behaviour on the part of Elaine would fit in with Marguerite's opinion that her daughter-in-law was a madcap and had not been a good wife to her son.

And certainly Yvan wouldn't be hurt. Hadn't he just agreed to a divorce? Admittedly he had said he had agreed to it to make her happy, because her happiness was all he had ever wanted, but she suspected he had put it that way to make himself feel better about his change of mind. Such an inflexible person as Yvan would have to have a good reason for changing his mind.

So why shouldn't she go while she had the chance, leave the days of roses and wine behind for ever? They weren't made to last anyway. She released the brake and eased the car on to the road, drove to the end of it and turned right over the stone bridge. Through the village she went, hearing the bells of St Augustine's ringing for Vespers. The main street was full of puddles and the shadows were paler than they had been on Friday afternoon. At the petrol garage Marcel was at the pump, talking to the driver of a car while the tank was being filled. He looked up as Elaine passed and raised his hand to his forehead in his usual salute as he recognised her uncle's car. Elaine didn't wave back but kept her eyes on the road and put her foot on the accelerator to leave Chambourtin behind for ever.

The familiar line of poplars came into sight. This time their shadows were hardly discernible against the twinkling wet surface of the road because the sun had gone behind a cloud. As the road curved away from the river in a bend she recognised only too well Elaine glanced automatically in the rear view mirror and gasped with shock. Behind her, coming at speed, was the grey Citroën, actually moving out to overtake her as she drove into the bend, a dangerous manoeuvre because there might be another vehicle coming round the bend the other way.

She pressed her foot down further, and the Peugeot leapt forward with a screech of tyres, sliding a little on the wet tarmac. Hands gripping the steering wheel tightly, Elaine turned it to guide the car round the bend. She wasn't going to drive into the ditch this time, she thought grimly.

Another car, going in the opposite direction, appeared and she felt her heart kick against her ribs and her mouth go dry. A quick glance in the rear view mirror brought relief. The Citroën had moved in behind her again. But it was very close, so close that she could see who the driver was—Yvan—and he was alone.

Using the opportunity provided by yet another passing car she accelerated more, but so did the grey car. She could hear the Peugeot's engine beginning to rattle and she knew she couldn't expect it to go any faster. It was beginning to rain again. Drops spattered against the windscreen and she switched on the wipers.

The road straightened out. There was nothing coming the other way, so the grey car moved out from behind her and came alongside and stayed there tormentingly beside her, making her nervous so that she couldn't steer straight because she was so busy glancing sideways to make sure the cars didn't touch. Ahead she saw another car approaching. Now the Citroën would either go ahead or fall back behind her again, she thought; but it didn't. It stayed right beside her, and in a panic because she was sure it was going to collide head on with the approaching car Elaine ran the Peugeot off the road on to the shoulder, braking as she did so. The car skidded and swung round, coming to a rest facing back the way it had come with its rear end slanting down over the bank and its headlights pointing to the sky.

Shaking as much with anger as with shock, Elaine switched off the engine of the car and tried to open the door. Since the car was on the slant the door was difficult to push open, and she was still struggling with it when it was jerked back out of her hand.

'Running away again?' Yvan's voice was coolly ironic, but there was nothing cool about the expression in his eyes as he glared down at her. There was nothing of the sophisticate about him either. He looked what he was, a rough, tough man of the earth, as strong as the rock that he was named after as he stood there in his stained blue denims. And he was angry, furiously angry. But then so was she.

'What were you trying to do?' she exclaimed. 'Trying to overtake on a bend and then staying out in the middle of the road when something was coming the other way!'

'I was trying to frighten you,' he retorted. 'Looks as if I've succeeded too. Where do you think you were going?'

'Paris, then England,' she replied, shaking her hair back from her face. 'You can't stop me.'

'I have,' he said dryly, making a gesture in the direction of the Peugeot. 'And you're not going on with your journey. You're coming back to Chambourtin with me.'

'No, Yvan. What's the use? We've said all there is to say. You've agreed to a divorce and that's all I needed to know.'

'I wasn't thinking about the situation between you and me,' he replied with a sigh. 'I was thinking about doing everything properly, according to the rules. You can't keep running, Elaine, just because someone says something you don't like. You've got to grow up some time.'

'I am grown up,' she protested.

'Then behave as if you are and come back to Chambourtin with me. As his nearest surviving relative you owe it to your uncle to be at his funeral, to be present when his will is read.' He paused and his lips thinned. 'You've no idea, have you, of how much you upset everyone when you ran away the last time; how worried everyone was at the chateau when you didn't return that evening last December? My mother was worried in case you were lying by a roadside somewhere injured. I had to go out and scour the countryside between here and Angoulême to look for you.'

'You did? But you weren't at the chateau. You were supposed to be in Cognac...'

'I've already told you I'd left there early to go and buy you a birthday present. So I was at the chateau too, waiting for you to come back and just as worried as the rest when you didn't come,' he said quietly. 'And now you're intending to put us through all that anxiety again. Why? Because you didn't think? Just as you didn't think that day when you were in Solange's apartment and saw my lighter and gloves. You didn't think about anyone else, only about yourself and how hurt you were. You didn't think about me.'

Rain was falling heavily again, adding to the perpetual rustling sound of the poplars. It was spotting Yvan's faded shirt and spangling his ruffled hair with glittering drops. Elaine could feel it hitting her bare arms, running down her face. Or was the moisture she could feel on her cheeks tears running from her eyes? She raised a hand to wipe it away.

'I'm sorry,' she muttered, 'I didn't mean to hurt anyone else or cause them worry, but . . . if only you knew how hurt I was when I saw those things, and when I heard you agree with her today . . .'

'What's this?' he challenged her, his hands on her arms as he shook her a little. 'You say I agreed with her?'

'Yes. When she very cleverly made out that I'd misinterpreted what she said last year because I didn't understand French very well, you believed her! You said: "*Mais oui,* that could be." You believed her and not me.'

'So you turned on your heel and ran,' he scoffed, 'and didn't hear what else I said. Ah, *chérie,* how many times does it have to happen before you'll learn? Always through your own impetuosity you're hurt. If you'd stayed a minute longer you'd have heard what I said next. Do you want to know what I said now?'

'Yes,' she whispered.

'Then let's get in the other car. We're getting wet standing here. We'll phone Marcel from the chateau and ask him to rescue the Peugeot for us. I expect he'll be very amused.'

He put an arm round her shoulders and together they went to the grey car. As soon as they were both seated in the front Yvan started the car, turned it and began to drive back towards Chambourtin and Elaine didn't object. He had taken over again, the devil she knew, the devil she loved and who possessed her in every way.

'To continue,' said Yvan as with one hand he selected a cigarette from a packet in the breast pocket of his shirt and lit it, 'I said that although I agreed you could have misinterpreted what Solange had told you last year I very much doubted that you had, because you'd been speaking and listening to French since you were a small child. You see, I knew she was lying again. I knew she had lied to you last year. I also know now why she did. I realised why, suddenly, when she walked in today.'

'Oh! Why did she?' she asked, turning to look at him.

'Because I turned her down,' he said flatly.

'Turned her down? But I thought you bought one of her pictures.'

'I did. It wasn't her painting I turned down. You see, that day when I went to her studio to see the painting she became suddenly very forlorn and told me how much she had missed me over the years she had been away, and regretted that she'd come back too late and that I was married to you.' His voice hardened scornfully. 'She suggested that we should have an affair, pick up where we left off. I refused.'

'And she felt scorned,' said Elaine, remembering what Marguerite had said about Solange.

'*Oui*. And she was able to take her revenge on me sooner than she could have hoped,' he went on, his voice edged with bitterness as he turned the steering wheel to guide the car round the bend where she had ditched the Renault. 'You turned up later the same day and she told you a heap of lies about my mother, about me and about Chambourtin. If you'd stopped to think then and had come to me and told me what she'd said I could have put it all straight for you. I could have told you all you've learned this weekend. But you didn't, and I still don't know why. Why didn't you trust me, Elaine?'

They were passing Marcel Daudet's garage now. There was no car at the petrol pump and the yard was deserted in the rain. The flowers in the window boxes looked limp and bedraggled after the afternoon storm. Elaine was beginning to feel as they looked, she thought with a touch of humour, limp with emotional stress, bedraggled because she had been caught in the rain, but somehow she had to answer this persistent question of Yvan's; find a reason in the recesses of her mind, face up to it, confess it.

'I . . . I was hurt,' she began. 'So hurt that I didn't know what to do; didn't know what I was doing, actually. We'd been happy, you and I . . . at least I'd been happy, and I thought you were too. Living with you, being near you every day had put me in the seventh heaven, a place I'd never hoped to find myself, so when Solange said you'd been visiting her . . . and insinuated that you were still her lover . . . I couldn't bear it. You see, I . . . I'd married you because I loved you, and to find out suddenly that you didn't love me was just more than I could take, I suppose . . . and I ran away.'

Her voice died away to a whisper and stopped. Yvan didn't say anything at first, but she felt the car leap forward as he accelerated and looked out to see that they were through the village and passing the church. The tyres screeched as Yvan took the turn towards the bridge too fast and then they were on it above the grey dimpling water of the Duvay. On the other side of the bridge he slowed down and guided the car off the road on to a triangle of grass just opposite the opening to the road which went to Bellevigne. In the silence which followed his turning off the engine Elaine could hear the faint swishing sound of the river as it slid past the banks and the patter of raindrops on the roof of the car.

Suddenly Yvan hit the steering wheel with his clenched fist.

'The filthy lying bitch!' he ground out between set teeth, and swung round to face her. 'She set out deliberately to wreck our marriage because she was jealous of you. But you said just now you married me because you loved me. What sort of love is it that crumples and dies when it's put to the test, as yours did?' He snapped two fingers of his uninjured hand mockingly. 'I give that much for such love!'

'Well, at least I married for love, which is more than you did,' Elaine retorted furiously. 'You married me because my uncle arranged it. That's something Solange didn't lie about.'

'Arranged it? Ah yes, you said that before. You said also that he'd bribed me to marry you. Where did you get such a strange idea?' he drawled, staring at her with narrowed eyes.

'I . . . I take back what I said about bribing you,' she muttered, 'because I know now that he possessed nothing he could bribe you with. But I know he arranged our marriage, because he told me he did yesterday.'

'The only arranging he did, as far as I know. was to invite you to come and stay at the chateau last summer for your holidays. We met and the rest followed as the night follows the day. We were attracted to each other and duped ourselves into believing we were in love . . .' He broke off and turned away to stare out of the window.

'You did the duping, I didn't,' she protested, 'out there in the woods. You made me believe you loved me, and now that I know you had nothing to gain by marrying me I can't understand why you bothered, why you didn't just take me that day when I offered ...'

She broke off, gasping, because he had turned on her savagely and had grabbed her to shake her violently.

'You don't understand, that's been your trouble all the time,' he yelled at her furiously, his anger bursting through at last, 'I married you because I loved you, because I didn't want our relationship to be a brief affair or a few snatched moments of sexual pleasure in the woods. I wanted it to be more, to have a chance to develop into something deeper. That's why I asked you to marry me first.' He let go of her suddenly, put his elbows on the steering wheel and clasped his head in his hands. 'Ah, *mon dieu*, you drive me beyond the bounds of all reasonable behaviour,' he muttered, 'so that I found myself striking you and shaking you.' He gave a stifled laugh. 'I even offered to let you have a divorce because I love you so much that I can't bear the thought of you being unhappy married to me.'

Quivering in reaction to his violent outburst, Elaine curled against the back of the seat, her eyes wide with alarm. Then slowly the sense of his words began to penetrate her mind as the faint ray of sunshine had penetrated the kitchen at Bellevigne after the storm. He had loved her and he still loved her and he had said so. But there were still questions to be answered before she could touch him, before she could put her arms round him and confess her own love for him again.

'If you loved me why didn't you follow me to England and ask me to come back, instead of waiting three months and then writing that horrid little note?' she asked. 'Oh, Yvan, if you'd known how unhappy I was waiting for you to come and tell me you wanted me back, to tell me that you loved me!'

He was still and silent, his head bowed, his long fingers thrusting through the tousled, wavy, grey-streaked hair. At the sight of the ragged towelling bandage on his right hand Elaine remembered she had been going to re-bandage his wound, but she had run away instead.

The silence was stretching into minutes, so she tried again.

'I suppose to explain would be to strip your soul bare and you wouldn't do that for any woman, not even for me, your wife, just as you wouldn't admit that you've been unhappy too,' she said quietly, then sighed resignedly. 'All right, it doesn't matter, but I'll go on wondering and not understanding, imagining the reasons why you drink too much, why you didn't follow me to England and reacting to what I imagine. I can't help it if you won't share your thoughts and feelings with me.'

Yvan moved and leaned back to look at her. A slightly mocking smile curved his mouth but his face was pale and haggard with the stress of the emotions he had just expressed.

'It was pride, pride and fear,' he said abruptly. 'Both of them stopped me from following you and dictated "that horrid little note". I was hurt too, you know. By running away without an explanation you struck at my pride in myself, my integrity as a person, and I was damned if I was going to run after you. I thought you'd come back.'

'Arrogance,' she accused.

'Maybe it was. On the other hand maybe it was just simplicity. You see, I believed in the vows we took in church and I thought you did too. Although my faith doesn't have the same name as your uncle's it's based on the same beliefs. So I gave you time to think and then wrote and asked you to come back, but I was afraid when I wrote, afraid to put my feelings on paper in case you rejected them.' He reached out a hand to push back the hair from her face and leaned towards her. 'Do you understand now, *ma mie*? I'm not a very complicated person, I have simple tastes and habits. When I met you I fell in love for the first time in my life, and I did what my father did when he met my mother, I asked you to marry me. There was no other reason, no arrangement with your uncle, although I know he was glad about our marriage and liked to think that without his invitation to you it would never have happened ... Now what's the matter? Why are you crying?'

'Because I'm happy,' she sobbed. 'Oh, Yvan, why haven't you said all this before?'

'Because you've never asked me before,' he retorted softly, leaning so close that his lips were very close to hers. 'You never cared enough to ask.'

His tongue licked the tear drops from her mouth and she flung her arms about him to hold him close, parting her lips beneath the pressure of his, tangling her fingers in his hair, then touched his face and slid her fingers down his cheek under his jaw to his throat, down to slip within the unbuttoned opening of his shirt to curl her fingers against the crisp hairs on his chest. And when he lifted his mouth from hers and pressed his lips against the hollow of her throat she whispered in his ear,

'*Il y a longtemps que je t'aime*. It's a long time that I've loved you.'

'Then why didn't you come back sooner? Why have you wasted nine months of our lives?' he countered, raising his head to frown at her.

'Because I didn't know how much I loved you until I saw you again. Maybe I had to be parted from you for a while to find out about the devil I know,' she murmured, and raised her face to his. 'Oh, kiss me again, Yvan, hold me, never let me go again.'

'I would like to kiss you and hold you and never let you go,' he said softly, his mouth tormentingly close to hers again, 'but I'd prefer to do it in more comfort than this. Where shall we do it? At Bellevigne or at the chateau?'

Elaine felt excitement leap along her nerves when she met his glance and saw in the dark blueness of his eyes that burning expression she had seen earlier.

'I'd like to go to Bellevigne,' she leaned her forehead against him, suddenly shy of the way he was looking at her, 'but I suppose we'd better go to the chateau in case they're wondering where I am. And you're expected to be there tomorrow anyway. Monsieur Léger is coming to read the will at eleven o'clock.'

'Then we'll go there,' he said. 'But first ... this.' Fingers under her chin, he raised her head. His kiss had the same bruising, dominating quality of the night before, giving her little chance to respond, as if he were punishing her for staying away so long. When it was over she was breathless and shaken, leaning against his shoulder for support.

'I don't much care any more why you ran away from me,' he said unsteadily as he stroked her hair. 'You're back now, but if you try to run away again you can be sure I'll be close behind you and I'll make you come back.' He pushed her away from him and reached out a hand to the ignition. The car started and soon it was purring along the road to Chambourtin.

'I suppose you learned that the company owned everything from Léger?' he said crisply.

'Partly, and partly from your mother,' Elaine replied. Her handbag was open on her knee and she was trying to comb her hair. 'Why didn't you tell me on Friday when I accused you of marrying me so that you could be co-heir to it with me?'

'I was tempted to tell you because I was so amazed by your accusation. I'd no idea, you see, that you knew so little about your uncle's affairs. Then it occurred to me that I might be able to use your belief to persuade you to agree to the pretence at reconciliation.' He laughed mischievously. 'A few well-chosen words and you were ready to agree to anything to prevent me from being sole heir. *Non, chérie,* don't attack me now, we might end up in the ditch.'

'But you could have told me about Bellevigne,' she retorted, sinking back in her seat.

'I didn't think you'd be interested,' he replied coolly, and she realised suddenly how cold and uncaring she must have seemed, not only to him but also to everyone else.

'It's a nice old house. I think I can make it look very attractive . . . that is if you'll let me,' she said humbly.

'Does that mean you've turned down my offer of a divorce? Does it mean you're prepared to settle down to being a placid French wife, cooking the meals and dusting the furniture?' he teased.

'As long as you don't go looking for pleasure in another woman's bed,' she taunted back gaily, feeling suddenly at ease with him in a way she had never felt before.

'Now why should I want to do that,' he replied softly, 'when I can come home to find you in my bed and know that you can give me all the pleasure that I need?'

'Honestly, Yvan?' she whispered.

'Honestly, Elaine,' he replied, and flashed an unexpected smile in her direction as he turned the car through the old archway into the courtyard. 'Oh, damn,' he added, seeing the two cars parked there, 'my sisters are both here. That means we shall have to be polite and show ourselves. It means a delay before we can be together, really together, *ma mie*. Can you wait?'

'If you can I can,' she said, still a little shy at being so open with him on sexual matters. Then she noticed the bandage on his hand. 'Oh, your hand!' she exclaimed. 'They're going to ask questions about it.'

'And not only about that,' Yvan said grimly as he stopped the car and turned off the engine. 'They're going to be curious about us. This morning I told my mother our reconciliation was only make-believe.'

'I know, she told me. What shall we do when we go in? Shall we tell them?' she asked, and watched his mouth curve tauntingly.

'I think I'd prefer to keep them guessing,' he grinned. 'Do you think you can pretend for a few hours not to be reconciled, just for fun?'

'I'll try, but it won't be easy, because I keep wanting to touch you,' she whispered, even then leaning towards him and offering her mouth invitingly.

'I know,' he murmured, his glance slanting to her lips as he touched her breast fleetingly, 'but remember, *chérie*, waiting will make it even more pleasurable.'

They went into the house, and Jacques appeared, to tell them that Marguerite was in the salon.

'You go up and change your clothes while I get Jacques to attend to this cut for me,' urged Yvan practically. 'I'll see you later in the salon.'

He went off in the direction of the kitchen with Jacques and Elaine went upstairs to strip off her skirt and top and kick away her wet sandals. Quelling her rising spirits, she selected a black and white dress which was the only one she had which was suitable for mourning. She rolled on a pair of sheer black tights and thrust her feet into shiny black high-heeled shoes. She brushed her hair and tied it back with a black ribbon, but didn't put on any make-up. Then, satisfied that her appearance was suitable, she went downstairs and along the corridor to the salon.

In the oblique light of the satin-shaded standard lamps the room looked at its best. The dark mahogany wood of elegantly curved chairs, the glass doors of dainty armoires, the rosewood of the old harpsichord in the corner, all gleamed with a subdued opulence and the green and gold of the Aubusson carpet, which showed signs of wear in daylight, took on a hint of its original luxuriance.

Marguerite was seated on the green and gold striped sofa which was placed on one side of the huge marble fireplace and both her daughters were seated there too. On the other sofa facing them sat two men, her sons-in-law. Between the two sofas on a long, low, intricately carved table was a silver tray bearing two decanters of sherry and some glasses.

'I'm glad you're back, *chérie*,' said Marguerite when she saw Elaine approaching. 'I was beginning to worry. You remember Paulette, Louise, Gilles and Bernard? Gilles, pour some sherry for Elaine, *s'il te plaît*.'

Elaine sat on the edge of a straight-backed chair and answered inquiries about her health from her two sisters-in-law and in turn asked about their children, all of whom, it seemed, had been left at home that day. She took the glass of sherry offered to her by Gilles and sipped from it.

'Was all well at Bellevigne?' asked Marguerite suddenly.

Elaine nodded. 'Yes, Yvan has come back with me. He'll be with us in a few minutes.'

'I'm glad he's come,' said Marguerite, 'we can have dinner all together. It isn't often I have all my family about me.'

'It's a pity that something sad had to happen before *that* could be arranged, Maman,' said Paulette. She was tall and dark like Yvan and her dark eyes expressed dislike as their glance rested briefly on Elaine's face. Elaine could guess why Paulette disliked her too, it would be because she had apparently deserted Paulette's beloved younger brother.

The conversation staggered along stiffly in a very un-French fashion until Yvan came into the room at last. He had washed and changed and looked sophisticated once more in his checked trousers, a dark blue shirt and his navy blue blazer. And suddenly they were all talking at once, chattering rapidly with many gesticulations, indulging in the French lifelong passion for talk. More sherry was poured for everyone and was drunk before Jacques appeared, to announce that dinner was served, and they all went through to the dining room.

She was glad they all had plenty to talk about, Elaine thought as she spooned up her soup. It meant that they ignored her. How different the meal was from the lonely one she had taken last night when she had been so unhappy, believing that Yvan was with Solange. She looked up as she thought about him. He wasn't saying anything either but was listening to his sister Louise as she told him about some escapade that one of her children had been in. He was listening attentively, obviously interested, and for the first time she saw him as his family saw him, as a good kind man.

Aware that she was staring, she looked away quickly, afraid she might have given herself away, and caught Marguerite's glance resting on her in puzzlement. Then Gilles, who was sitting beside her, asked her a question about London and she turned her attention to him.

When dinner was over they all had coffee in the salon. The chatter went on until Paulette rose to her feet and said it was time she and Gilles set off for La Rochelle, as it was a long drive. Turning to Elaine, she held out her hand.

'I'll say goodbye,' she said. 'We shan't be coming to the funeral, and I expect you'll be going back to England afterwards.'

In the sudden silence while everyone's eyes turned to her Elaine felt sweat prick her skin. How accusing they all looked, as if she were guilty of a great crime, and she supposed to their way of thinking she was; the crime of deserting her husband. She wanted to cry out that it was none of their business whether she was going back to England or staying on, but she knew they wouldn't understand.

'I . . . I don't know yet,' she stammered, 'I'm not sure. It's been nice seeing you again, and you, Gilles. Thank you for coming.'

Paulette's eyes seemed to glint derisively as Yvan's often did before she turned away, and the difficult moment passed. Half an hour later Louise and Bernard left and Marguerite announced that she was going to bed.

'Are you staying the night here or returning to Belevigne?' she asked Yvan.

'I'm staying here,' he replied coolly, 'so that I'll be

present when Monsieur Léger comes. *Bonsoir,* Maman.'

Marguerite frowned, glanced from him to Elaine and then back to him again.

'I see you have hurt your hand,' she said, pointing to the white bandage.

'It's nothing.' He shrugged his shoulders.

'I'm glad you came back this evening with Elaine,' she said, 'it made all the difference to Paulette and Louise. I wish . . .' She broke off and turned away to go up the stairs. '*Bonsoir,* Elaine. *Bonsoir, mon fils.* I shall see you tomorrow. Maybe then you will tell me the secret which is giving you so much joy.'

They waited until she had gone from view and then they stepped towards each other. Hand in hand they went up the stairs in silence to the tower bedroom. They did not switch on the light because the room was lit intermittently by the moon, which was playing hide and seek among the clouds.

As soon as he had closed the door behind him Yvan pulled Elaine into his arms and claimed her lips in a fierce stifling kiss.

'I think my mother has guessed,' he murmured at last.

'I think so too,' she said, turning around so that he could unzip the back of her dress. 'I'm afraid I gave myself away at dinner.'

'How?' As the dress unzipped he put his arms around her inside it, his hands cupping her breasts lightly as he touched the side of her neck with his lips.

'I stared at you for too long,' she said with a little laugh, and stepped away from him. 'And when Paulette said goodbye I didn't know what to say. I wanted to tell her it was none of her business whether I stayed or not.'

'Thank God you didn't,' he replied, 'she would never have understood.'

He took off his jacket and tossed it on to a chair and loosened his tie and pulled it off. Shirt and trousers followed the jacket and he came round to the side of the bed where Elaine was twisting her way out of her tights. When she straightened up he smoothed the unzipped dress away from her, every movement of his hands a caress. For a moment they stood breast to breast in the moonlight, their lips just touching, then suddenly he lifted her on to the bed.

'Now let's see whether it was worth waiting for,' he challenged softly as he lay down beside her and gathered her against him.

An hour later Elaine lifted her fingers lazily through his tousled hair as Yvan lay with his head against her shoulder.

'Was it worth waiting for?' she asked softly.

'What do you think?' he murmured sleepily.

'I think it was, but I hope you won't mind if there are any consequences.'

'What do you mean?' he queried, raising his head so that he could peer at her.

'After last night and tonight we might have a child,' she said.

'*Mon dieu,* I didn't think!' he exclaimed, and suddenly they were both laughing.

'Oh, *chéri,* I'm so glad there are times when *you* don't think either,' cried Elaine, winding her arms round him again. 'Did Uncle Armand ever tell you about his dream, that he would like us to have a child who would be heir to Chambourtin?'

'*Oui,* he told me on Friday night when I sat with him.' He paused, then added quietly, 'But I hope you're not going to imagine that that's why I made love to you last night.'

'Oh no, it didn't occur to me! After all, Chambourtin wasn't his to leave to anyone any more,' she said seriously. 'I hope you've forgiven me for imagining all those horrid things about you,' she added in a low voice.

'I'll forgive you for that if you'll forgive me for last night,' he countered. 'I couldn't help myself ... after all those months of being without you, and then to find you so close, so desirable ...'

'Shush,' she said, 'there's nothing to forgive. I wanted it too, even though you said today that love didn't come into it.'

'I said that because I wasn't sure of how you felt,' he responded.

'But you know now, don't you? Oh, please say you do, Yvan, because it's true. I loved you last night, I love you now and I'll love you for ever, and I'll never run away again.'

'Because you're never going to get the chance again,' he said roughly, and as their lips met in the darkness Elaine smelt the scent of roses and wine that wafted into the room through the open window from the courtyard below, and knew with a wild singing happiness that the days of roses and wine weren't over after all, but would be hers for evermore.